Books & Bribes

A Cozy Witch Mystery

Book Store Cozy Mystery Series

Lucinda Race

MC Two Press

Editor Kimberly Dawn
Cover design by Mariah Sinclair
Manufactured in the United States of America

First Edition March 2023
Print Edition 978-1-954520-44-8
E-book ISBN 978-1-954520-43-1

Authors Note

Hi and welcome to my world of cozy mystery. I hope you love my characters as much I do. So, turn the page and happy sleuthing .

If you'd like to stay in touch, please join my Newsletter. I release it twice per month with tidbits, recipes and an occasional special gift just for my readers so sign up here: https://lucindarace.com/newsletter/ and there's a free cozy mystery when you join!

Happy reading...

Pembroke Cove, ME

1. Robin's Cafe
2. Bygone Antiques
3. The Pembroke Cliffs
4. Cozy Nook Bookstore
5. Twisted Scissors Hair Salon
6. Betty's Market
7. Old Town Libary
8. Miss Judy's Dance Studio
9. The Sweet Spot Baker
10. Bee Bee's Boutique
11. Tuckers Hardware Store
12. The Copper Kettle
13. Police Station
14. Town Hall

Chapter 1
Lily

QUICK NOTE: If you enjoy Books & Bribes, be sure to check out my offer for a FREE novella at the end. With that, happy reading!

***

Achoo. A thick cloud of dust flew up from the pages of the hefty book that had fallen off the shelf. It barely missed my head as it hit the floor with a *thump*. I stumbled backward over a small stool and let out a scream as I tried desperately to catch myself on anything before falling.

A sandpaper-like feel scraped over my cheek from the wooden floor and I slowly opened my eyes. There was Milo, my gray tabby cat, hovering over me. I scratched his long, soft coat. "Hey, little man. I'm okay. Just took a tumble." I eased myself to a sitting position and gently rubbed the back of my head where it had connected with the floor. Not a great way to end a Monday.

A deep gravelly voice said, "You've been lying there for several minutes. I didn't think you'd ever wake up."

I looked around. "Who's there?" My heart rate increased as I scrambled to my feet and grabbed the heavy book. As I hurried down the aisle of the bookshop, scanning right and left, I wondered who was in my store. I was certain I'd locked the front door at four on the dot after my last customer left.

I checked the empty sitting area in front of the oversized north-facing windows with two wingback chairs, a small table between them, and a round table in front of them. It was great natural light for reading. But I was alone.

Shaking my head gingerly, I surmised it must be the residual effect from hitting my head. Glancing at the fat blue book in my hand, *Practical Beginnings*, I decided I'd climb the stepstool tomorrow and find a place for it. Walking back to the wide wooden counter, I dropped it on top and stroked Milo's soft fur. "Ready to go home?" My besties were meeting me at the library for classic movie night. Tonight was *Death on the Nile* by Agatha Christie, and I didn't want to be late.

I had locked the cash register when I heard a scratchy, but kind voice say, "Ready when you are."

With the stapler in my hand, I twirled around, shaking it in the air. "I demand you show yourself!"

"Lily, it's me. Your old buddy Milo."

"Stop it. Right now!" Who was in my shop?

"Look at your cat," the voice urged.

My heart thudded in my chest. Was something wrong with my sweet baby? "Milo?" I scooped him into my arms and held him tight.

"Need. To. Breathe." He squirmed in my arms and escaped to the counter.

I stumbled back against a long table stacked with bestsellers. Some dropped to the floor as my weight sagged against it. "Did you just speak?" The words came out as a croak.

"I've been waiting for you to open that book for ages. Remember Aunt Mimi asked you to read it on your last birthday?"

I nodded, dumbfounded. This couldn't be happening. I could hear him, but his tiny mouth wasn't moving. I lifted my hand and grazed the slight bump on the back of my head. My cat was talking to me. Wait, I must have hit my head harder than I thought or worse, had something possessed me? I rubbed the back of my head again. Ouch. "No, I must be concussed."

I walked around the room, checking to make sure the windows were secured and double-checked the front door was locked. "Yup, all tight as a drum."

"We already knew that." Once again, it was the same voice. My legs jiggled like rubber. I dropped to the chair and put my head between my legs just in case I felt faint. After a few seconds, I sat up. This was stupid. I was having a conversation with a prankster.

"Milo, if you're really talking, come over here and sit in this other chair."

I watched as he walked to the edge of the counter and dropped to the floor, only to hop up in the chair opposite me. This couldn't be happening. No way he understood.

Licking his front paw and rubbing it above his eye, he said, "Now what do you need me to do for my next parlor trick so that you'll believe me?"

"Tell me what I'm thinking?" I leaned closer, giving him full access to my face. The close proximity would help me see if his mouth was moving.

"I'm not telepathic. I'm your familiar and

yes, that means you're a witch. Finally, the truth is out." He stretched over the cushion and rolled on his back as if I was supposed to scratch his tummy. "Feel free."

Like always when Milo rolled over, I obliged by scratching his belly and his eyes would close in contentment, but this time he was giving me directions where I should be scratching.

"If you're going to be bossy, I'm done." I went to stand up and dropped back in the chair. "Wait, what did you say about being a witch? I own a bookshop. There is nothing special about me."

My cat opened his eyes and he rolled to his side, never bothering to blink. "You can believe that's nothing special, but a few witches live in Pembroke, and you are one of them."

Once again, I felt as if I had fallen from the stool and conked my head, but I was sitting on a comfy chair, talking with my cat who just announced I was a witch. "Wait." My thoughts were spinning. "Does that mean Aunt Mimi is one, too?"

"Stop repeating yourself, and now you're catching on." Milo jumped to the floor and looked up. "I thought you said we were going home. I'm hungry."

My breath came rapidly and my head swam. This couldn't be happening. I must be dreaming. As I bent over to put my head between my knees, which seemed to be the thing to do again, a tapping on the glass in my door drew my attention. Who on earth would stop by now? I looked at my watch. It was almost five. Again came the insistent knocking.

I got to my feet, albeit unsteadily, and waited until I felt I could plaster a smile on my face before going to the door. When I peeked out, relief washed over me and my breathing slowed. Why I was being such a nervous Nellie was beyond me. Must be all this talk of familiars and witches. With a glance over my shoulder, I jabbed a finger in Milo's direction. "Shush."

"No one else can hear me. When I talk, they hear a cute little meow coming from my tiny mouth."

I frowned. "Tiny is debatable at this point." I pulled open the door. The minute I saw his handsome face and dreamy hazel eyes, my knees went weak. It was one of my oldest and dearest friends and also the guy I'd been in love with my entire life. Gage Erikson.

"Hi there. I was expecting to see you later at the library."

Gage walked in and looked around. "I thought I heard you talking. Are you alone?"

Heat flushed my cheeks. This wasn't something I was about to share with anyone, having a conversation with a cat and he talked back. I forced a grin and added an extra dose of cheeriness to my voice. "Just talking to Milo. There's no one else here."

Gage bent over and scratched between the kitty's ears. Instead of a purr, she heard, "Hmm, that feels good. Thanks, Detective Cutie."

There was no reaction from the man, so at least there was that. Milo opened one eye and I would swear the cat winked at me.

"Gage, what brings you around? Did you

want to drive to the movie together?" I clamped my mouth shut. That sounded way too much like a date and I didn't want to do anything to make our friendship awkward so I rushed ahead with, "Nikki and Steve are meeting us there and maybe even Aunt Mimi and Nate O'Brien."

"Sounds like it's going to be a packed house." He looked at me while he scooped up Milo to continue giving the kitty attention.

"I guess." Seeing Gage holding Milo was like kryptonite to me, causing my heart to do all kinds of crazy flips. Anyone who loved someone else's cat had to be a keeper, right? I sighed, and his brow quirked.

"You okay?"

"Oh. Yes. I fell off the stool earlier and hit my head."

Concern filled his golden-hazel eyes. He deposited Milo in the chair and took a step in my direction. "Where did you hit it?"

My hand went to the tender spot on the back. "I'm fine."

"Turn around so I can take a look."

I did as he asked, enjoying being fussed over a little, but not wanting to appear like some weak girl who needed his attention like those girls at the coffee shop. They were always giggling whenever he walked in, especially when he used to wear his police officer's uniform. He pushed ever so slightly on the spot that connected with the floor and tears sprang to my eyes and I cried out, "*Ouch.* That hurts!"

His laugh was comforting. "Guess I found the spot. You should put ice on it and take it easy for tonight."

I turned back to face him. "I can't miss the movie. It's one of my favorites."

"Mine too, but that's why I stopped by. I can't make it tonight. I have to cover a shift for Mac Sullivan. His wife's gone into labor and we're short a man."

"That's exciting. About the new baby I mean, not about you working." I had to hold my disappointment in check again so as not to appear as anything more than a friend. "We'll miss

10

having you there to chow down on popcorn and red licorice."

Gently he tucked a stray lock of my hair back behind my ear, a motion he had done thousands of times. But it made my heart race. I kept my eyes glued to the old oriental carpet in the middle of the room. No way was I going to let him see my eyes. He was way too perceptive and would see how I felt about him which I've spent years hiding.

"Maybe I'll swing by tomorrow around ten with coffee?"

When I looked into his eyes, I wondered if I saw a flicker of hope that I would say yes. Which I would, about anything. Dang it, in my head I sounded like a freshman in high school with a crush on the football star. "That'd be great. But if you're bringing coffee, any chance you can get one of those pecan buns, you know, with extra icing?"

"Is that your way of asking if I'll stop at the Sweet Spot?"

"Well, you offered coffee, and they make the

best pastries in three towns." I playfully batted my eyelashes just because I could and knew it always made him laugh.

Right on cue, he grinned. "That can be arranged." His cell rang, and he glanced at the screen. "I gotta take off. Duty calls."

He dropped an almost kiss on my cheek on his way out the door and called over his shoulder, "See you in the morning." And then he was gone.

After a long sigh escaped my body, Milo said, "Really? Do you think he does not know that you're into him?"

Turning my back on him, I said, "I will not start talking to my cat about my love life."

Milo trotted in the direction to where I stored his cat carrier. "You mean your nonexistent love life, don't you?"

"Milo?" I meant for it to come out as a warning to hush up, but it sounded more like a question to my ears. "Do you think Gage knows I have a crush on him?"

"Yeah. And if you opened your eyes, you might see the feeling is mutual."

When I finally got to the library a little after six, the usual group had gathered in the community room to watch the film. My best friend Nikki was there with her boyfriend Steve, and my aunt was there with Nate. Marshall Stone was running the projector and Teddy Roberts and Jill Dilly were there too. The group was rounded out with a few teenagers from the high school and a couple of new faces. Typically, there'd be a few more stragglers before the film actually got started. This was shaping up to be a fun evening.

I waved to Meredith across the room, one of the librarians who worked there. She was a quiet woman, with a long blond braid down her back and round wire-rimmed glasses giving her a studious look. With a shy smile on her face, she returned my wave and looked at her boss, the head librarian, Flora Gray. She was bustling about, making snide comments about how tomorrow, she'd be vacuuming up popcorn, candy wrappers, and heaven only knew what else from the floor. She was not a fan of movie night.

"Flora?" I stopped her as I helped set up the chairs. "Why don't you join us tonight? It's a classic Agatha Christie."

Her eyes narrowed and she glared at me. "I'm a librarian. That fact should be enough to explain. I prefer books over any other form of entertainment. Especially when it's in black and white." She lifted her chin as disdain dripped from her words.

She didn't need to be so snarky. "I was trying to include you so you'd see what a wonderful group of people attend."

Meredith passed by, her arms loaded with books. "Flora, you know the movie buffs always leave the room immaculate. I don't think there is any need to be so harsh on Lily."

Flora gave Meredith a withering look, and she hurried to the other side of the library. Flora wiggled a large keyring in front of me. "I'll give this to your aunt, and she can lock up. But I'll be back later tonight to check on things. Everything had best be in place. And for once, clean up after yourselves." She pointed to the dish of hard candies on the side table. "Get rid of those. They draw ants."

I did not understand where she was coming from. Our group never left a mess. In fact, we cleaned the restrooms and the small kitchenette every month. It was odd she pointed out the candy dish since I did not know who brought it. But it didn't matter; the place would be spotless before we locked up. "Don't worry, Flora. I'll make sure everything is clean and tidy."

She jabbed a finger that almost touched my chest. "See that you do."

I watched the older woman march out of the room. Through the doorway I kept an eye on her just in case she came back for round two. Her short steel-gray hair was in a no-nonsense style. She always dressed exactly the same way. A starched white blouse, a horsehead broach, and black slacks with sturdy tie shoes. In the winter, she added a fisherman knit sweater to stave off the stiff ocean breeze as she biked from her home to the library. Even in the snow, she still biked. I could never figure out how, since the winds of the water were enough to push a car around, let alone a biker. I often thought she looked like the wicked witch from *The Wizard of Oz*, riding her bike in the tornado. But it was none of my business. At least I took comfort in knowing she treated everyone the same as me. She was an old biddy and thought she was doing the town a favor by letting groups hold events there.

At one time, Flora had tried to put an end to our gatherings. Even though she was on the board of elders, the rest of the group had intervened and reminded her it was a public space and community-minded groups could use it as long as it was on a schedule.

Pushing all thoughts aside, I turned my attention to Nikki, my best friend for life. We were complete opposites. She had long strawberry-blond hair while mine was dark in a pixie cut; her eyes were blue and mine, brown, and we always had each other's backs. She held up the DVD for Marshall to see.

As she grew closer and smiled at me, she asked, "What did the old bat complain about tonight?"

Marshall looked at us and said in his best Sherlock Holmes voice, "Fair to say, everything. I swear, how can someone as cantankerous as her even want to live in our fair town?"

Standing over six feet and strong as an ox, he owned and worked a vegetable farm on the outskirts of town. Years in the sun had left him with deep creases in his weatherworn face. Marshall had been running the projector for the last five years and, like everyone in Pembroke it seemed, had at least one run-in with Flora. The last time she had been downright vicious when she thought he had broken the projector. It turned out all that was wrong was he had unplugged it at the end of the night.

People had taken their seats and the lights had just shut off when I heard Aunt Mimi scream, "*Help*! Somebody help!"

Chapter 2
Lily

I ran from the community room, scanning the space as I raced through the library. Where was my aunt? Panic clutched my throat and squeezed my heart with each step I took. She screamed again as if she was in agony and it cut to my core. I burst through the front doors and skidded to a stop on the top of the granite steps. Aunt Mimi was standing over Flora's motionless body. A blood-covered baseball bat was in my aunt's hand. I recognized it was the kind Little League kids use. Lying next to her crumpled body were several books, a candy wrapper, a brown paper sack, and her tote bag. "Where did you get the bat?"

"It," she stammered, "it was leaning against the handrail, and it started to fall. I didn't want it to clonk her in the head, so I grabbed it."

That wasn't something I wanted to hear. If it turned out to be the murder weapon, which based on the amount of blood it was, Aunt Mimi's fingerprints were on it. "Put it back exactly as you found it, okay?"

She carefully propped the bat against the railing. Holding her hands out, palms down, as if she was steadying herself, she said, "It was just like that."

I nodded to show that I had heard her. I saw Teddy, Jill, and Marshall standing at the front of the group and Teddy was stuffing something into his front pocket. The rest of the movie buff fans had followed me from the community room. I didn't want Aunt Mimi or anyone to mess up the evidence. I had watched enough mysteries to know we needed to call the police. "Touch nothing."

"Do you think she's," Aunt Mimi's voice dropped to a hoarse whisper, "dead?"

If the situation hadn't been dire, I might have laughed at the way she said the word. Like it was contagious or something. "I'm not sure." I didn't want to touch Flora, but someone needed to see if she was breathing so when the police were called, they'd know to send an ambulance and not a hearse.

I walked down the steps, giving the crime scene a wide berth. "Flora, can you hear me?" But she didn't move. A pool of blood had formed under her head. I was extra careful to avoid that mess since it wouldn't do if I stepped in it. Besides contamination of the evidence, it was yuck. I didn't want to have to throw out my cute penny loafers; they were just broken in. I glanced at my aunt and thought, thank goodness she couldn't read my mind, worrying about my shoes. But she was frowning at me. That was odd. I needed to check if Flora had a pulse.

The bump on the back of my head twanged from where I had bonked it earlier as I leaned forward. I placed two fingers where her carotid artery should be thumping. Again, thank you, Netflix, for the tutorial. Nothing. Her skin was warm which made sense as she had just left less than fifteen minutes ago.

"Aunt Mimi, call Gage. He needs to get down here, but tell him we need the funeral home, not an ambulance."

Nate rushed to her side and while she was talking, I took a closer look around. There was a butterscotch hard candy wrapper next to her right hand and keys looped around her left fingers, but not in a defensive position at all. If it wasn't for the bat and the blood on the back of her head, one could surmise she died from a fall down the stairs.

Minutes later the wail of sirens was growing closer and I couldn't quite see what was underneath her. It almost looked like a red rose. Was that even possible? I never heard of any man who would give Flora anything, let alone flowers.

Car doors slammed and Gage ran to where I stood. "Lily, are you okay?"

I appreciated that his first concern was for my safety. I pointed to Flora, who lay in front of us, definitely dead. If she hadn't been, she would have been yelling at all of us for gawking. She was one who wanted to be center stage when she was hurling snark at others. Being hurt, or in this case worse, didn't matter.

"What happened?" He touched my arm. It was a familiar touch that calmed me. "Were you the one to find Flora?"

He hadn't needed to feel her pulse. Another officer, Sharon Peabody, a rookie I had met a few weeks ago, had done that the moment they'd arrived. She informed Gage in a monotone voice there was no pulse.

"Aunt Mimi screamed, and we were inside. The movie was about to start and you know how it goes, talking and microwaving the popcorn. Just as the lights went out, I heard the screaming, and I came running. I found Flora like this and told my aunt to not touch anything and made sure everyone heard me, too."

I looked back at the group of onlookers. Marshall, Jill, and Teddy were clustered together. The teenagers had formed a close-knit circle away from the movie buffs and the newcomers stood off to one side. My eye caught Meredith hovering in the doorway, wiping her eyes with a hankie. I gave her an encouraging smile, hoping to convey everything would be okay.

Gage walked around, guiding me to step to one side so Peabody could take some photos. He nodded with a knowing smile. "Netflix again?"

My heart skipped. "You know me so well."

Officer Peabody cleared her throat. "Detective Erikson, I'll tape off the area and request an investigation unit." She waited for Gage to agree with a nod.

I pointed to the bat. "I think that is the murder weapon, but why leave it?" I was talking more to myself than to Gage, who was still beside me, but his focus had turned to the scene in front of us.

"Lily, this isn't a game of Clue or some old movie. Don't start spinning theories."

I didn't look at him so I wouldn't have to fib.

There was nothing I loved more than solving a good riddle. Crossword puzzles, Jenga, scavenger hunts. If there was a puzzle to solve, I was the *it* girl. And for the first time I had a real-life—well, dead—mystery I could try my hand out on.

"Gage, give me a little credit. I know this is serious." I was going to have to be very careful as I poked around. Then I had an interesting thought. I had an ace in the hole, a confidential confidant. Milo. There might be some advantage to being a witch with a familiar after all.

A while later Gage sent everyone home. I walked Aunt Mimi and her decades' long boyfriend, Nate, to their vehicle. The movie was forgotten in all the excitement. As we approached Nate's truck, I broached the subject of the book. The one that caused me to fall.

"Aunt Mimi, do you remember that book you asked me to read?"

Her eye twitched, and she glanced my way

and then back to the stone path we were walking on. "Yes."

"I opened it up today, and it was full of dust. Where did you find it?" Even if she wasn't looking at me, I was keeping my eye on her. After all, I had just discovered she might be a witch too, and she was the sweetest woman in the world. Now, that was an interesting comparison. The sweetest woman found the most cantankerous one dead tonight. What were the odds?

"Everyone has read it in our family over the years. Did you read any of it yet?"

The little minx was being awfully coy. "No, in fact, I left it at the bookshop when I took Milo home."

She stopped short and tipped her head. "How is Milo?"

"Chattier than ever."

She nodded. "It happens from time to time with a cat. They grow with us. Look at me and Phoenix. We've been together forever."

That was an interesting statement and come

to think of it, Phoenix had been alive for as long as I remembered. "How old is she now?"

Aunt Mimi's eyes darted to Nate and then to me. "I don't remember, but she's in perfect health and who knows, she might even outlive me."

This was interesting. "Anyway, tomorrow I'm going to start reading the book and see if there are any puzzles in there to solve." I adored Nate, but right now I wished it was just Aunt Mimi and me strolling along. I could pump her for information.

"How about if I stop around midmorning and we can chat? I might shed some light on where you should start reading."

Nate piped up. "Most people start at the beginning, my beautiful mermaid."

She slipped her arm through Nate's. "And sometimes it's best to let the book tell you where to start. It adds to the thrill of life."

What was my aunt trying to tell me? That this book would guide me on the alternative path to my future? "Gage is coming around ten, so stop in a little later."

She gave me a sly wink. "I'll bet he's stopping at the bakery, too." She waved her hand. "No need to confirm the truth. I'll come down around noon and we can have lunch. I want to hear all about coffee with Detective Cutie."

"Aunt Mimi, don't call him that and Gage is not my guy." Not that I wouldn't open the door if he came knockin', but that was a pipe dream. It had been too many years since we'd been tap dancing around each other and eventually some girl much prettier than me would catch his eye and he'd be a goner. Me? I was a one-man kind of gal.

"We hear you talking, but neither of us believe that's true. But we can talk about that tomorrow, too."

We reached the truck and Nate opened Aunt Mimi's door. She kissed both my cheeks and placed her cool hand against my warm cheek. "Please don't worry about a thing. I promise everything will make perfect sense in time."

Nate gave me one of his special bear hugs and told me to drive safely. He didn't say it, but I knew it was on all our minds. There was a murderer on the loose.

As I watched them drive away, I noticed Jill Dilly sitting in a parked truck in the passenger seat. I didn't recognize the vehicle, so I wandered in her direction, waving as I went. Thank goodness it was still light out. I didn't want to scare the poor woman.

"Jill, what are you doing out here by yourself?"

"Oh, hello, Lily. Marshall drove tonight. We take turns, you know, each driving in for movie night. Living outside of town, it just seems to make sense."

I scanned the small parking area. But Marshall was nowhere to be seen. "Why didn't you wait in the library?"

"With all that commotion and knowing that Flora, no matter how vile she was..." Her words stilled on her lips and her face was white and drawn. "Someone offed her, while we were just a short distance away." She shuddered. "And Lily, how are you so calm? You actually touched her body. I saw you."

I thought this was an interesting take on things. Jill actually seemed to be more weirded out that I touched Flora rather than the fact someone had killed her. "It wasn't like she was going to get up and start yelling at me."

Jill shook her finger at me. "You're just a little too glib about all of this for your own good. You'd best be careful and mind your business, like Gage said. I know you think you're some kind of amateur sleuth, solving the mystery of the missing popcorn or blurting out the ending of the movie before we've all had time to figure it out."

"I like to exercise my brain. There's no harm in that."

She pulled her mouth into the tightest scowl I had ever seen. "Marshall's coming." She gestured out the windshield and sure enough, there he was. But unlike Jill, he seemed to be almost happy. A song lyric flitted through my head— ding-dong, the witch is dead. Now that was odd. Walking beside Marshall was Teddy Roberts, followed by Nikki and Steve and a few other people from movie night.

Nikki lifted her hand in greeting. "Hey, Lily. Want to come with me and Steve? We're going to swing by Robin's Café for some cake."

My friend never had a piece of cake she didn't like and just as the bakery had the best sweet rolls, the café had the best cake, especially this time of day. "Thanks, but no. It's been a long day and I think I'm going to head home and spend some time with Milo. He was acting a little weird today." I held back a snort. That was the understatement of the century. But first I was going to swing by my bookshop and pick up that book, *Practical Beginnings*. With what little Aunt Mimi said, I was curious to see what else Milo might know about it. I guess that was enough mystery for me right now.

"If you change your mind, stop down." Nikki

and Steve walked off in the direction of the café. They both lived above the shops on Main Street and walked almost everywhere. Convenient for the lovebirds, too.

Marshall and Teddy each nodded in my direction before they got into Marshall's truck. I guessed more than two people carpooled to movie night. "Take care, guys."

I waved and wandered to where I had parked. Someone must like butterscotch candies. I bent over to pick up the wrapper. It tempted me to go back to the steps of the library just to see if there were any more clues, but no. I needed to go to the shop and then home. Gage was right, I loved a mystery, but I had more than enough on my hands with this whole idea of living with a talking cat and my aunt having a cat that was at least forty years old.

Book in hand, I hurried up the front walk, eager to get out of my work clothes and into comfy yoga pants and an old tee shirt. I slowed as I approached the door, wondering why the screen was in place, but the inside door was standing wide open. I paused on the top step and listened, straining to hear if there was someone inside. But all I heard was silence. I closed my eyes to think. Could I have not closed the door all the way and the breeze nudged it open?

"It's about time you got home, Lily."

I stood on the bottom step. Who the heck was talking? Milo. I placed a hand over my racing heart and took several long, slow, deep breaths. "Milo," I hissed. "What if someone hears you?"

"I'll sound like a cat, remember? Call your buddy Gage and have him come over. Someone left you a present on your kitchen table. But don't worry. It's wrapped in brown paper, like the kind my fish comes in on the rare occasion you buy me a treat."

"Someone walked into my house and left a gift?" No, that didn't have a nice sound to it at all.

Milo sat back on his haunches. "I wouldn't call this a gift, more like a clue."

Now he had my undivided attention. "What is it, and who was it?"

"I don't know everyone in town, so I don't know who it was. They were dressed in black, wearing a mask. Like I said, it's wrapped up. But as your familiar, it's my job to look after you, so before you get too curious, call Gage."

"I'm just going to take a quick peek."

Milo got up and swished his tail. Before he disappeared into the kitchen, he said in a haughty tone if cats can sound that way, "Don't say I didn't try to help."

I rubbed my hands together. My first clue. And I was officially investigating my first ever murder case.

Chapter 3
Gage

I looked around Lily's perfectly maintained lawn as I approached her cottage. My adrenaline was pumping. When she called to say someone left something on her kitchen table and she thought it was a clue to Flora's murder, I couldn't get to her home fast enough. First thing, I wanted to protect the only girl who stole my heart years ago, and I didn't want it back. And I knew Lily; her curiosity was killing her right about now.

I raised my hand to knock, but the screen door opened and there she was, those soulful brown eyes and pert nose with a smattering of freckles with a sprinkle on her cheeks too. The girl of my dreams, but it was too bad she didn't give me the time of day. But I'm not giving up. Someday she'll see me for more than just her good friend.

As I stepped into the house, I bumbled my words. "I came as fast as I could, considering I was at the scene of a crime." The words died as I noticed her face was bright with excitement. Not what I had been expecting. Lily was actually grinning like she had just won the prized teddy bear at the summer carnival. This was not good at all.

She took my hand and I couldn't help but notice how well they fit together. She tugged on it, indicating I should follow her. When we got to the kitchen, on her table, I saw a large box wrapped in brown paper, just as she had said.

"Look. I think it has to be a clue to Flora's..." Several beats passed until she said, "Murder."

I walked around the table, inspecting the package. It was about sixteen inches square and the paper had Lily's name stamped on one side. I peered closer and there was actually a cat stamp, too. How curious. "You haven't touched it yet?"

She shook her head, but her eyes still sparkled. "No. I waited for you, but if you hadn't come soon, I was going to open it."

I just looked at her, thinking she was brilliant on one hand, but on the other, it was easy to see her enthusiasm got the best of her. Along with her inquisitive nature, it was double trouble. "Glad you erred on the side of caution. Which is unlike you. Why did you wait?"

She glanced at Milo and if I hadn't known better, I'd swear he shook his head in my direction. But cats only understood a few phrases from their human. Dinner, treat, and another treat.

"I don't know." Her singsong answer now really had me wondering what was going on here.

"How's your head? From today I mean?"

She rubbed the back and a small frown graced her lips. "A little tender, but no headache." She gestured to the box. "Can we rip the paper off like it's my birthday and see what's inside?"

"Only you would think a package left by an unknown person is exciting." I wanted to laugh since I too wanted to open it, but we needed to be cautious. I approached the box. Before picking it up, I pulled a pair of latex gloves from my back pocket and put them on. This would help to preserve any evidence. If we were lucky, there'd be fingerprints. "Let's take this out back, just in case."

Lily held open the back door and I carefully lifted the box and inspected the bottom, noting it wasn't heavy. I walked out back to her deck and set it on the bistro table. "The top and bottom are securely taped."

"I'll get scissors."

Before she went in the house, I pulled out my Swiss Army knife from my front pocket and held it up. It had all the tools we'd need for this operation. "We're set, bubbles."

She smiled as my old nickname for her

slipped out. I had promised her when we were in high school that I wouldn't call her that anymore, but darn, in this situation, it fit.

Lily's eyes were wide as I sliced the top. Her nail clicked against the tabletop as I went slowly to preserve the paper in one large sheet. "Patience."

Holding out her hand, she said, "Give me the knife and I'll do it. We could be here all night at the rate you're going."

I gave her a side-glance. "You will not tamper with evidence. I should have just taken the box down to the station and asked you to forget you ever had it."

With a snort, she said, "Yeah. Right. Like that would happen. I'd discover what was inside." She crossed her arms over her stomach and a slight pout formed on her soft pink lips. Reminding myself I had a job to do, I refocused.

I folded the paper open to the sides. The cardboard top had one piece of scotch tape holding it together. An easy slice. Next was sparkly tissue paper. Whoever they were, they had gone to a lot of trouble.

"What do you see?" She stood on tiptoes, trying to peer inside.

There was a handwritten note. Holding it by the corner, I pulled it out and scanned the paper. What the heck? "It's signed, Flora Gray."

Lily held out her hand. "Can I see it, please?"

"Nope. I'll hold it and you can read it. I don't have an extra set of gloves."

A frown came and went on her face in a second. She read aloud.

Lily,

If you're reading this, I'm dead. Which means I need for you to stick your nose into my business and figure out who killed me. The police are incompetent, and I've had my eye on you for years. I know you're the only one who can solve the case. Well, maybe you could ask your boyfriend, Gage Erikson, to help."

Sincerely,
Flora Gray

The sparkle that had been in Lily's eyes dimmed. "I'm sorry she said the police were incompetent. I don't feel that way. But isn't it great that she recognized my talent for solving puzzles? After all these years to discover she may have actually liked me."

I went to put the note back in the box when she said, "Wait. I want to get a picture." She pulled her cell phone from her pocket and took pictures before I could protest.

"I'm done. You can put it away now."

After I secured the note in the box and folded the paper up, I said I was going to put the box in my truck and I'd be right back. We needed to have a serious talk about her inserting herself into my investigation.

Lily had the Keurig turned on when I made my way back to the kitchen from the front door. Milo had taken that moment to come with me. I'm sure he was hoping for a treat and since I knew where she kept the tin, I helped myself to give one or maybe two to the fur ball. I had to wait until I had Lily's full attention before trying to talk about the case and how she would not be a part of it. She moved around her kitchen and soon had set out not just piping hot coffee, but a small plate of my favorite no-bake cookies.

"Now, where were we?" She smiled from across the table before getting up again. "Be right back."

She hurried down the hall and came back with a notebook. This did not bode well for my planned conversation about her hanging up her sleuth hat. She held the pen at the ready.

"Now, tell me everything you found at the scene of the crime."

I sipped my coffee and selected the largest cookie on the plate. "Nope. Not happening."

"Aw, come on. You heard what Flora said in her note. She thinks I'm the only one who can solve the crime." She looked at Milo and said, "Isn't that right, Milo? I have skills we haven't even tried out yet."

The cat yawned and looked bored. Like this

people stuff was annoying him. He lay down on the rug in front of the kitchen sink and stretched out, making himself appear almost twice his normal length. What a life. If there was such a thing as reincarnation, he was coming back as Milo. And when I gave it another thought, that was one sure way to be with Miss Lily Michaels.

"Why are you grinning?"

Lily's question interrupted my train of thought. I needed to think fast. "Seeing how excited you were over opening this box was," I paused, "illuminating." She must have been satisfied with that because she stirred cream into her coffee and lifted the mug to her lips. "What do you make of Flora's note?"

She had gone into her puzzle-solving mode. A telltale sign, she chewed the corner of her lip as she twisted her mouth into the cutest half smile and wrinkled her nose. It had been like this in school when we were taking exams—total concentration. Not looking at me, she sipped her coffee. Finally, she said, "She knew she was in danger and I think she knew the possible suspect." She set her mug down and folded her hands on the tabletop. "But why didn't she come to you? I'm pretty sure she found you the least objectionable cop in the department, confirmed by the simple fact she said I should consult with you."

My laugh came out more like a bark. "Don't you find that funny? The police are incompetent, but you, a bookshop owner, could solve it, with help from me."

Lily lifted her shoulder and smirked. "If the badge fits, wear it."

Clutching the middle of my chest, I groaned, "How you've wounded me."

Her laughter was musical and despite the seriousness of the conversation, being with Lily was the best part of my day. But I needed to stay focused. There was a murder for me to solve, but no one had said I couldn't consult with a friend who just happened to have a brilliant mind.

"Let's get back to the subject of Flora. Did you notice anyone out of the ordinary hanging around the library tonight? Like someone who hasn't come to movie night before? Or possibly when you found your aunt over Flora's body?"

She closed her eyes as if she were looking at pictures. Milo jumped up in her lap and she petted him absentmindedly. "We had some new people, but Flora didn't acknowledge them. I have a sense that something wasn't quite right, yet I can't put my finger on it." She opened her eyes and looked at me. "One thing I found odd was Jill Dilly, Marshall Stone, and Teddy Roberts all drove together. When I asked Jill why, she said they take turns since they're so far out of town." She narrowed her eyes. "But that makes little sense. In all this time, I've never seen them carpool."

I couldn't see why she would think it was odd.

"They had Marshall's truck, but Teddy lives closer to the docks, not inland."

This was something I needed to jot down for when I talked to Teddy tomorrow. Why had he hitched a ride with Marshall when he would have been driving in the opposite direction? "Did you see what direction they went in?"

Her lips flattened into a straight line. "No, sorry."

"Let's talk about those first moments after you got to the top of the stairs. What did you see?"

"Aunt Mimi's face was beet red. I'm sure that was from screaming. She pointed to Flora and as soon as I saw the blood, I looked around. That's when I saw the bat and someone needed to know if she was alive. Since no one else was looking to do it, I touched her neck to see if I could find a pulse, but nothing." She tipped her head. "Did you see the candy wrapper?"

"I did. But who knows how long it had been lying there."

"What kind was it? Just for giggles." I was curious to see how observant she had been.

Lily had something she was processing, and I didn't mind sharing the detail. "Butterscotch."

She nodded but said nothing more about the wrapper. It was as if she had made her mental note to be mulled over later. "And was there a flower under her body?"

"Actually three. A red, a yellow, and a white rose."

"That doesn't make any sense. Red is for romantic love, yellow for friendship, and white is purity. When I saw the red, I thought maybe this was a lovers' quarrel gone bad." She broke a cookie in half and handed me a piece. Never one to turn down one of her cookies, I happily accepted it.

"But if it was something in the romance realm, why the white and yellow?"

I was of no help when it came to flowers. I knew you gave long-stemmed red roses on Valentine's Day and a guy could never go wrong with pink. That tidbit was confirmed when I gave Lily pink roses on her last birthday.

"Had anyone mentioned Flora was dating?"

She rolled her eyes in my direction. "Please. Flora was like a vampire. She arrived at the library before the sun came up and never left until after dark."

Tapping my index finger on the table, I stopped mid tap. "Then why did she leave early tonight?"

Lily's face lit up. "Unless it was to meet her boyfriend, and they had a tiff. He lost his temper, swung the bat after he had given her the flowers. So, with the force of the blow, she fell face-first, crushing the flowers beneath her." She brushed her hands off like they had dirt on them. "Case solved."

"I can tell by the way you're beaming you're pretty proud of yourself, but there's one minor problem."

She arched a brow and gave me an inquiring look. "Such as?"

"The baseball bat was not an object of convenience. It had to have been brought to the library, so this was premeditated. Not a crime of passion."

Her face dimmed, and then she perked up again. She popped her index finger in the air. "Unless a kid had left it behind and the scorned lover grabbed it and clocked her a good one.

You know how Flora could be totally exasperating."

Milo meowed. She ran her hand down his back. "What's wrong, Milo?"

He let out the most mournful cry, and Lily looked at me. "Can we talk about all of this tomorrow? I think all this talk of murder has upset my fur baby."

What? Cats can't understand humans, but Lily looked like she was exhausted and after the day she had with hitting her head and then Flora, it was understandable she needed some rest. I got up from the chair and Lily walked me to the door. As my norm, I bussed her cheek with a reminder I'd be by at ten.

"Good night, Gage."

As she was closing the door, it was crazy, but I could have sworn I heard her ask Milo, "So who was Flora dating?"

Chapter 4
Lily

I scooped Milo up and carried him to the kitchen. After what he had just said about Flora, he deserved some of the special lactose-free kitty milk I gave him on rare occasions. I had so many questions, it might just loosen his tongue. After setting the shallow bowl on the floor, I waited impatiently until Milo had lapped it all up.

"Spill it, kitty. How do you know Flora had a boatload of cash stashed at her house?"

He gave me a disdainful look. "I'm a cat, right? I wander around our tiny little town and I see things. Nobody censors themselves around animals. They think we can't understand humans."

That was when I knew Gage's remark stung a bit. "You should cut Gage some slack. How's he to know that you comprehend every word?" I waved my hand in the air. "We're getting off track. Tell me what you know so I can figure out what to do with it."

"Don't you think we should talk about your newfound witchery? It's so much more interesting than someone who was taking money from a bunch a people."

I was torn. I wanted to know more about my new circumstances, but I also wanted to help Gage solve this murder and Flora explicitly asked me to help too. The town didn't need the publicity, being on the verge of a summer season. Tourists brought in a lot of money to the economy. Including into my bookshop.

"Can my newly discovered identity help me in this situation?"

Milo looked me up and down, as if assessing what he should tell me. "Potentially."

It came out more like a purr, which I found oddly encouraging. "Then let's start with my being a witch." I figured I'd start with a straight-forward question. "How many witches live in Pembroke?"

Milo rolled on his side. "That's for me to know and you to find out."

"You sound like a bratty kid on the school grounds." I thought about what else I wanted to know. I brushed the hair out of my eyes. Ideas were bubbling. "I know Aunt Mimi is a witch. She kind of gave that away tonight when she talked about the book and told me where to start reading. But are all the women in our family witches?"

He groaned and put a paw over his eyes. "Men can also be witches, but some prefer to go by warlock or wizard. It really is a personal preference."

I prodded the paw with my finger. "And?"

"Lily, you'll find all of that out in time. For

now, maybe you should ask what you can and cannot do."

I jumped up and paced the kitchen, my frustration increasing as Milo seemed to be determined to evade my questions. "Why did I choose you at the shelter? On some level, did I already know I was a witch?"

"Now you're asking better questions. I was chosen for you to teach and guide you through your journey. And I'll always be with you."

"Cats don't live forever." But then I thought of Aunt Mimi's cat, Phoenix, and her longevity.

"Now something clicked. You know, I can always tell when your mind puts the pieces together."

I flopped onto the chair. My head was aching and a gentle throb was behind my eyes. This could turn into a full-blown migraine if I wasn't careful. "Tell me everything I need to know, and we'll call it a day. Then first thing tomorrow, you can tell me about the moncy."

Milo got to all four paws, arched his back with a slow spine-stretching motion, and padded down the hall with me following. "Read the book. I'm going to bed. You've exhausted me today."

"Wait." But with a swish of his tail, he disappeared into my office. I was sure he'd curl up in the window seat and sleep until morning. I couldn't believe I was standing in the hallway, listening as a cat told me to read a dusty old book. It wasn't the worst idea. First, two aspirin and a cup of tea to keep me awake. This might just be a long night.

The next morning, I woke to Milo lying on my chest, purring. I squinted against the bright sun flooding the room. I forgot to close the blinds before snuggling into bed. Wait. Milo was purring. That means yesterday was some kind of crazy dream. Maybe even Flora's murder was a part of it.

"Milo, you'll never believe what happened yesterday. It all started when a book full of dust made me lose my footing."

"I was there, remember?"

I bolted upright in bed, flipping him from my chest, and he rolled across the bed. "You can talk?" That's when I realized it wasn't just a dream. I was a witch. I had a familiar. And Flora Gray had been murdered just feet from where I had been sitting.

With a flick of his tail, he stalked from the bedroom. I must have offended him, but I'm sure it wasn't going to be the last time.

My cell phone text message tone, a foghorn, blared. It was from Nikki, and she wanted to talk about the murder and what I planned to do to solve it. I sent back a question mark and decided I'd better get dressed and take my tired bones to my shop. Gage would stop by with coffee and the caffeine was just as much of a pick-me-up as seeing him.

"Milo!" I called out. "Are you coming to the shop with me today?"

Either he was really miffed at me or had gone for a morning cruise around the neighborhood.

I had dressed in just tight enough jeans to show off my figure, just in case Gage took a second look. I added a pretty lavender floral blouse and matching cardigan. I was almost ready to go, but I couldn't find my loafers. I searched high and low, but they were nowhere to be found. I wore them yesterday.

"Milo. Are you hiding my loafers to get back at me for forgetting that you can talk?" Not that it would do any good since he was more than likely giving me the silent treatment or outside.

I padded into the kitchen in my bare feet, determined to find them when I did a double take. Milo was sitting in the middle of the table as if he was waiting for me.

"First lesson." His voice was not a sweet little purr, but more like the growl of a hungry lion.

"I don't have time. I need to get to the shop."

He glanced at my bare feet. "Without shoes?"

Ah-ha. So he *did* have something to do with their disappearance. "I'm going to wear my sneakers." A good thing that just popped into my mind.

He nodded in the direction of the chair. How smart was this cat? I wanted my loafers. They went best with my outfit. Grudgingly, I took a seat, but he had like thirty seconds to confess or I was outta here.

"Did you read any of the book last night?"

I could feel heat flush my cheeks, but as much as I wanted to fib, I didn't. "No. I fell asleep as soon as my head hit the pillow."

"Close your eyes and think of where you took them off. See them in your mind."

I did as he asked, even though I felt ridiculous. As much as I wanted to not see them, I could. "I took them off at the front door." My eyes popped open, and I leaned forward, hands clasped on the edge of the tabletop. "But I've looked and they're not there."

"Of course not. I moved them as your first lesson in spells. This will be a very simple location spell and what I'm about to teach you will help you find your other things. A more difficult version will come later, after you've perfected this one."

I closed my eyes again. "Okay, what's next?"

"That's better," he said. "Now take several deep breaths and I want you to think about what kind of being you'd like to use as your guide to finding lost objects."

I squinted with one eye and looked at Milo. "Why can't I use you?"

"You can. But some people use a wiseman or woman, as this just represents that part of your mind which sees all."

It was settled. I was using Milo, or the kitten version of him. "I'm ready."

"Take your time and ask your question silently. Again, open your mind and listen for the answer. When you see your shoes, remember to be humble and thank your guide. When you open your eyes, don't expect your shoes to just appear like a genie wished them in front of you, but have patience and shortly you'll find them."

I did as Milo instructed. At first, I could feel impatience gnawing at me, telling me I should get up and keep searching for my shoes. But after several minutes of deep breathing, I felt something shift inside. In front of me was a large escalator. I got on and rode it up. At the top, a sweet kitten was resting on a white couch. I scratched his little gray head. A mini Milo. The kitten wore a serene look, and then I softly asked to find my loafers. The kitten seemed to bow her head, and to the side was another escalator going down. I got on and rode to the bottom and I was back in my kitchen. Slowly, I opened my eyes and Milo was watching me with an intensity I hadn't seen before on a human, let alone a cat.

"I'm going to feed you and then get ready for work."

Milo jumped down and did a figure eight between my legs. He was acting almost like a normal kitty, or maybe he was just a little proud that I could sit still for five minutes.

I opened the cabinet where I kept his food and did a double take. Sitting on the bottom shelf were my loafers. Popping hands on my hips, I whirled around to ask Milo what the big idea was, but he was nowhere to be seen. All the same. It was still an excellent lesson. If I was going to be a good witch, my guess is patience would be important and since it had never been one of my virtues, I needed lots of practice.

Once I got to the shop, wearing my loafers but without Milo, I flipped the sign on the front door to OPEN and set up for the day. All the overhead and reading lights were switched on, the blinds up to let natural light flood the space, and I even brought the old book, *Practical Beginnings*, with me. If there was going to be slow time, I'd have something to occupy myself with.

I walked into the small kitchenette, which also served as my office and storage room, and had just stored my lunch in the refrigerator when Milo squeezed through the small kitty door. He walked to his water bowl and lapped up a long drink. I waited until he was finished before I asked, "Ready for questions?"

Moments later, he sat back and looked up at me. "Yes?"

"Where did you slink off to this morning?" I kept my tone even and unemotional, even though now that I knew he was smarter than an average kitty, I figured he could get into even more mischief.

"One of us had to get into Flora's house and check out a few things."

"Like what? The woman was a librarian and served on the Pembroke Town Council. She lived a pretty dull life." Then I thought about the boyfriend. "Maybe she didn't, since it seemed Flora had a secret love affair going on."

"Unless I've missed something at her house, there was no man in her life. Nothing shows anyone other than one person living or even being in the home."

"Wait. How did you get in?"

"At one time, she must have had a cat since there was a little door just like yours. It was unsecured, so I walked in. It was almost like an invitation."

"Milo, you should have told me where you were going. Anything could have happened to you."

"I'm a cat and unless I encounter another witch, no one will even give me a second thought."

He had me with that logic. "What else did you find out?"

He jumped to the chair and then the small table. "Come closer."

I looked in the direction of the front door. "There's no one here." But of course, I did as he asked. It seemed I was going to spend a lot of time doing as he asked.

"When I poked around in her bedroom, under her bed to be specific, there was a tote bag. And," he paused for dramatic effect, "there were bundles of money falling out and onto the carpet."

"She didn't use a bank. That's not a crime." So much for the big dramatic revelation. "I have to get out front."

"Lily."

The lionlike grumble had me stopping in my tracks.

"The stacks were wrapped and secured with rubber bands and all were exactly the same height."

Now he had my full attention. "Are you saying something smells fishy, and not just at the docks?"

"I think they were payments of some kind. You know, like you see in the movies when the perp is paying off the blackmailer?"

I laughed, picturing Flora as a blackmailer. She just wasn't the type and besides, who in our sleepy little town would have the kind of secrets that would warrant blackmail?

The bell on the front door jingled. I needed to get out front.

I heard, "Lily, are you in the back?"

Gage. My heart skipped a beat, and I tossed a look to Milo over my shoulder as I hurried out of the room. "We'll talk about this later."

"Better yet, ask your detective. I'll bet he knows if it's possible she could be doing something illegal. The cantankerous librarian was definitely up to something."

Before I stepped into the main area of my shop I had to wonder how I was going to bring up the subject of blackmail and bundles of money to Gage. It's not like I could say my cat told me.

Chapter 5
Lily

Gage was holding a pastry box in one hand and in the other a cardboard drink tray with two covered coffee cups. And he looked handsome. He was dressed in distressed blue jeans, a black long-sleeved tee, and cowboy boots. His light-brown hair was still damp, and I longed to finger comb it back into place.

"Good morning, sunshine." He smiled, which set the butterflies bouncing around my tummy.

"Morning, Detective." His eyebrow arched, and I laughed. It was such fun to tease him.

"I'm not here in an official capacity this morning. Just bringing my friend the promised treat."

I led him to the wingback chairs and small table. It would be easier to have a casual conversation about the case if we were both relaxed instead of standing over the counter. Hopefully, nobody would pop in to buy books this morning.

Gage flipped opened the box in one smooth motion and set it on the table. I took the cups of coffee from the tray and noticed my name was on one.

"French vanilla was the special today, so I got you one."

"That was sweet of you." How he wasn't dating anyone was beyond me. I took a sip and caught him watching me over the rim.

"Did you work on the case last night? You seemed to be in a hurry when you left and I figured you had to go back to the library."

"Correction, Lily. You rushed me out because you were concerned for Milo and I figured you were using him as an excuse since you had a pretty rough day. Speaking of, how's your head feel now?"

Now that he mentioned it, I put my hand on the back where the bump was yesterday, but other than a teensy bit tender, it had returned to its normal feel today except the lingering tenderness. "Good. More like a minor bruise."

I decided not to rehash the whole thing about who rushed who out of the house. "Did you have to go back?"

"No. I went to the station and read a few reports. When I leave here, I'm going to the library. We have officers inside going over the place."

"That must be a bit upsetting to the patrons."

He took a big bite of a bun and muttered, "We closed it down for a few days while we investigate. I consider the entire place a crime scene until we're sure there's nothing more to be learned."

I sipped my coffee, trying to broach the subject of the money at her house. "Any news on the boyfriend angle?" With his bun gone in a blink, I had to wonder if Gage was a witch making the bun disappear so fast.

"Not a clue to be found so far." He gave me that assessing look like when we're playing chess and I'm winning.

"Do you know something, Lily? And if you do, you need to tell me, especially if you think it will help the investigation."

"I don't think there was a man in her life. I've never even heard a hint of a peep." Nibbling on my bun, I casually said, "Maybe there'd be a clue about his identity at her house. If you want to go over there, I'd be happy to go with you and look around. You know, from a woman's point of view."

His laugh came out like a snort. "We have female officers on the force and Peabody can come with me if that becomes necessary."

"Peabody's new to town, and she certainly didn't know Flora like I did. Yea, she'd get it right from the procedures, but I knew Flora a long time. Growing up around here gives me some advantages." I lifted my shoulder in a small shrug as if it was no big deal, but my heart was hammering. I wanted in that house.

"No, Lily. I can't let you snoop. It's against regulation."

"It's fine, but if you change your mind, the offer still stands." With a new idea hatching, I wouldn't need his permission or help to get inside. There must be some kind of spell for opening doors. I smiled. This witch stuff might just be super handy.

Aunt Mimi came at noon on the dot carrying a picnic basket over one arm and wearing a long floral dress that went almost to the ground, a large-brimmed straw hat covering her long graying hair, and sunglasses that were dotted with rhinestones. She must have been using her Bedazzler again. Despite her age of seventy-odd years, she didn't look a day over fifty. Was that a perk of being a witch? I added it to my mental list of questions.

"Lily." She handed me the basket and hugged me with her other arm. Looking me up and down, she beamed. "Don't you look pretty today. Discovering you're a witch agrees with you."

This was how we were going to start our lunch? Not having any secrets between us anymore. I liked this fresh approach.

"Aunt Mimi. I'm so glad to see you."

She swept her hat off and fluffed up waves of silver hair. "I couldn't wait to get here and you have to tell me everything you learned last night from the book, and of course, Milo." She looked around. "Where is your familiar?"

I unpacked the basket, my mouth watering over lobster salad rolls, cutup veggies, two large chocolate fudge brownies, and a thermos of something equally delicious.

"Milo's in the back snoozing. He's had a busy morning. He was checking out Flora Gray's house."

Aunt Mimi's face fell. "That old biddy." Her shoulders dropped. "I shouldn't speak ill of the recently departed, but not many people will be brokenhearted over her passing. I've never met a more cantankerous human being in my life."

She withdrew clear plastic plates and cups but with cloth napkins and arranged our lunch. "Would you pour our tea?"

I went to unscrew the thermos when she placed a hand on my arm. "Dear, that is for non-witches. We use magic to do mundane things like this."

"I, um, well, I didn't get very far in the book." It pained me to say that I hadn't read anything and, based on her withering gaze, I knew she guessed the truth.

She touched her index and thumb together three times, like she was trying to snap her fingers when the top loosened.

"Since you seem to want to talk more about Flora than your new powers, we might just as well get it over with, and then you can focus on how your life has changed literally overnight."

I did not know how it could have changed that drastically. All I had done so far was see a focus on a tiny request to find my shoes and I discovered taking deep breaths really cleared my mind. But if Aunt Mimi said it, it had to be true.

"Is the lobster from Nate?"

Aunt Mimi fluttered her hands as the two plates seemed to float between them. "Yes, and he wanted me to tell you he's excited about your new life."

Now I was stunned. Nate knew about the witchcraft? He had been in love with Mimi for years, even if she wouldn't agree to marry or even live with him. They were still connected like the ocean and the tide.

"That's really nice of him, but how exactly is my life going to change that much?"

With a shake of her head, she said, "Lily. Lily. Lily. That is part of the reason you need to read the book. You can do things." She added air quotes to these last two words.

"Like Samantha on that television show?"

"Nose twitching isn't real, but snapping fingers and her concentration like when she puts her fingers on her temples, that is similar to things you might do. Of course, we won't know for sure until you try and—"

I finished for her, with no snark. "I know, read the book."

We enjoyed our lunch at a leisurely pace, talking about the food and Nate's lobster business. When the last lump of lobster meat had been consumed, she patted the corners of her lips with the napkin and with a flick of her wrist, the dishes stacked themselves.

My mouth fell open. If I hadn't been paying attention, I would have missed it. "Aunt Mimi, what else can you do? That was neat."

"I've had many years to practice. So, I can do a great many things, some useful and others just for fun."

That's when my brilliant idea hit. "Do you have a time turner?"

Now she just looked shocked. "A what?"

"You know, like in that movie, about the witches and wizards?" I couldn't understand why she was surprised I'd ask. That would be great in my arsenal as I helped Gage solve the mystery of who killed Flora.

"That's fiction." She snapped her fingers and stood up. "I'm going to work the shop for the rest of the day. You take the book and go to the library where it's quiet and study." She waved her hand in the direction of the door. "Off with you."

"One problem with that. It's closed because of the ongoing investigation." But a new thought came to me. If everyone was downtown, maybe that meant Flora's house was available for a quick look-see, and then I could read the book at home. I kissed Aunt Mimi's cheek and thanked her for watching The Cozy Nook. On my way out through the back, I looked at Milo. "Ready for a side trip before we go home?" I opened the back door, and he strolled through it. One thing about my familiar, he was up for this as much as I was.

.   .   .

Arriving at Flora's, it was just as I suspected. No one was around and even the birds were silent. Milo was sitting in the passenger seat as if he had been riding shotgun forever, but before yesterday, he rode in a cat carrier. It didn't seem right to me that I put him in one now. Plus, we could discuss the case as I drove.

"Here's what I think we should do." I began with a quick survey of the street. Making sure no one was around, I lowered my voice. "We sneak around to the back door and go inside. I'll take a quick run through the main rooms and you can show me where you found the money. We should be in and out in less than fifteen minutes."

Once again, his disdain for my plan was clear in his tiny little face. Who knew a cat had so many expressions?

"How do you suggest you gain entry?" He looked me up and down. "Trust me, we will not fit through the same door."

I hadn't thought of that. "Maybe it's not locked." I opened my car door and closed it softly. No sense in announcing our arrival. "Are you coming?" I looked at my feet, but where was Milo?

"Come on, poky. We're supposed to be sneaking in, remember?" Milo was waiting for me near the corner of the house at the end of the driveway. This was the first time I had ever been this close to Flora's house. The front lawn was tidy, with two perfectly shaped evergreen bushes next to the front door. But nothing was flowering. Other than the green, there was no color at all against the brown shake shingles.

I hurried to join Milo, but I didn't run just in case someone walked by. I didn't want to create suspicion as to why I was here at all. I looked over the side of the house too, hoping by chance a window was open and I could shimmy up and in. But not even a blind was up. A shudder raced down my back. It was as if the house was in mourning for its owner.

By the time I reached the back, I saw the cat door swinging. One of us was in. Now to try the door handle. I gave the screen door a tug, and it pulled open, but the knob on the interior door didn't turn in my hand. I jiggled it again, but it was definitely locked.

There had to be a key, but where? I closed the screen door and was getting ready to start searching anyplace that might be a hidey-hole for a key. I remembered my first lesson. Unsure if I needed to be sitting down or if it could be done in the standing position, I had nothing to lose, right? I closed my eyes and took several deep breaths that seemed to reach to my toes. Breathing in and out slowly, I really concentrated on each one. The same escalator from this morning appeared before me and I got on. This time the journey to where baby Milo sat on the pillows didn't take long. As I had earlier, I humbly asked where I could find the key to give me entrance to Flora's home. Once again, the kitten bowed his head, and I took the escalator back to my starting point, which this time was on the back steps.

When I opened my eyes, I forced myself to not get all impatient like I normally would, reminding myself to stay focused on the key. There was a small table and two chairs at the far end of the yard. There was a statue of a cat on a stack of books. I did not know Flora had any kind of fondness for any animal, so the statue caught me by surprise. I lifted it. No key. I replaced it, thinking I had been so sure when a new idea came to me. I tried to lift the cover of the cement book and sure enough, with a bit of pressure, it popped open and there was the key. After a little happy dance, I unlocked the door and tiptoed inside.

"Milo, where are you?"

"Right here." He stalked across the kitchen counter. "Good work out there, Lily. You might just make a decent witch, after all."

Taken aback by his praise, I smiled. "Thanks."

"Hurry and look around so I can show you the money and we can get out of here." He strode out of the kitchen with me close on his paws.

I made quick work of the tiny house and

Milo had been right, no sign of anyone other than Flora being here. When we got to her bedroom and I was on my knees, I saw a bag. "Does it have dark-blue handles?"

"Cats are mostly color blind, at least compared to what you might see, so I'm not sure."

I lay flat and wiggled partially under the bed. Using a pen, I was able to snag the handles and tugged it toward me. There were stacks and stacks of money and not small bills, but all hundreds. I had no idea how much might be there, but suffice it to say Flora didn't make this kind of money, being a librarian in a small town.

A heard a knock on the front door and I froze. This would not look good, me, in Flora's house, holding a bag of money.

Chapter 6
Gage

I noticed Lily's car parked down the block from Flora Gray's house. After I checked it out and saw her handbag and an old dusty book on the passenger seat, I had a sinking suspicion I knew where she was. My temper spiked, but I should have guessed she'd take matters into her own hands and poke around. There was a part of me that was impressed with the way her mind worked and she was following the clues.

I strode back to the house and rapped on the front door. Not that I expected her to answer, but more as a warning that she needed to know she was on the verge of getting caught red-handed. I didn't wait on the front step but jogged to the back door and leaned against the house, arms folded across my chest, just waiting.

A few minutes later, Milo came out the kitty door, and he locked eyes with me. He swished his tail and went back into the house. What was he going to do?

The back door cracked open, and she peered out and told Milo to head on home. How on earth would he understand what she was saying? But that was the least of her worries. I cleared my throat and her eyes connected with mine.

"Hi, Gage. I guess you're wondering what I'm doing here?"

"That is my first question." She gave me a sheepish smile and stepped onto the back step, carefully closing the door behind her.

"Well," she drawled, "I started thinking about Flora's boyfriend and, like I said, since I'm a woman, I'd be able to spot anything that might be male-oriented in her house." She shrugged as if it was no big deal that she had entered a locked house that was part of a murder investigation.

"You broke into a house." I straightened. Part of me was furious, but the other side wanted to know what she discovered.

She held up a silver key. "No, I didn't. I used this."

I covered my mouth and coughed to cover my laugh. "Where did you find a key? Officers looked everywhere last night and came up empty."

With a sweet, innocent smile, she pointed to the back of the yard. "See that cat and book statue? It was in there."

"And what made you look there, of all places? Most people look under the doormat." I knew for a fact it wasn't there. It was in the report I read last night.

She said something that I couldn't really understand, but it sounded like I would never believe her. "Lily, how did you know to look under the statue?"

"I didn't say under, but in." She crossed the

lawn and looked to see if I was following her. "Come on. I'll show you."

I'd follow her anywhere, so across the grass was a snap. "You never said what made you look here."

"A hunch and remember the cat stamp on the box?"

"Just another puzzle for you." I would love to see how her brain worked, but I wasn't about to tell her since I'm guessing she found more than just a key.

She touched the top of the cement book and flipped back the top, which, by looking at it, I would never have thought to do. "It was sitting right there." She dropped the key back in and closed the lid.

I held out my hand and said, "I'll take that."

Her frown turned into a playful pout. "But if I give you the key, how will I be able to get back in the house when I have a new idea?"

This time I laughed loudly. "The whole point is you're not supposed to get in. Key."

Her shoulders drooped, and she opened the

book again and placed the key in my out-stretched palm. Closing my fingers over it, I thanked her but could see it didn't set satisfacto-rily as the frown went from her lips to her eyes.

"I'll see you around. I'm going home."

I glanced at my watch. "Who's covering the shop?" And the bigger question I wanted to know was why she wasn't there. Lily was hard-pressed to take any time off. I should know; I've asked her to go fishing with me a bunch of times. Rarely does she accept.

"Aunt Mimi. I have a book I wanted to read, so she offered and I accepted."

Her tone was light, as if she did this all the time. But something was up. I just couldn't put my finger on it, yet. "Mind if I stop by later?"

"Suit yourself." She fluttered her fingers in my direction and jogged back to the driveway and out of my line of sight.

Instead of going in the front door, I wanted to go in the same way Lily had, to try and see the house through her eyes.

Closing the door behind me, I flipped the

lock. I didn't want to have any nosy neighbors wandering in. I stood still and scanned the room slowly as if there was a scrap of information just waiting for me to discover it. Lily would never disturb anything she might have found, but she seemed to have a sixth sense for the smallest detail that could turn out to be relevant. Like the cat stamp on that box. But the counters were bare, the sink empty, the table cleared, and the refrigerator front barren of notes. It was as if no one had ever lived here.

I walked into the living room and, other than a stack of Agatha Christie books, it too was devoid of a feeling of human occupants. The bathroom cabinets were next, and then I went into her bedroom. I stopped dead in my tracks. On the carpet there weren't vacuum marks, but it looked as if something had been slid back and forth over the carpet. Before I would get on the floor, I needed to check out the rest of the room. I opened dresser drawers, the closet, and even the wooden box on her dresser, which had a few pieces of jewelry and a scrap of paper with two rows of what looked like random numbers. I took a picture with my cell phone to figure it out later. The entire house was empty and not because the person whose name was on the mailbox was dead, but this was a house devoid of energy.

I took a deep breath. My instincts were screaming. I was about to get my first solid clue. Pushed back against the wall was a small cloth bag. I went around the other side and, using my pen, tugged the bag out from under the bed. Money fell out onto the carpet, and I pulled my cell phone out and took pictures. This was a lot of money for a woman who lived alone, with a stable job, but not for this kind of cash.

Sitting back on my heels, I had to wonder if Lily had found the bag or maybe she hadn't had enough time to find it. That was something I'd find a way to drop into the conversation tonight. I took a bunch more pictures and went back to my car to get a large evidence bag to take the money. This case just got a lot more challenging.

. . .

Later that night, I tapped on Lily's front door and waited until I heard footsteps growing closer. She pulled open the door, and she was in a ripped Maine sweatshirt, yoga pants, and fuzzy socks. Her hair was standing up in spots like she had been running her hands through it and not in an easy, carefree way.

"Hey." She left the door open and turned back down the hall.

I followed her, closing the door and leaving my shoes next to the bench. Glancing in the living room, there were mugs of what I guessed had been coffee and tea, a water glass, and a plate with a half-eaten slice of pizza. Whatever Lily had spent the afternoon working on had been intense.

"Hungry?" she called out as I strode into the kitchen. She was putting a slice of lukewarm pizza on a plate, then she handed it to me. It had been a rhetorical question since she knew I never ate at the department.

I sat down at the table and let the moments unfold. "How was the rest of your day?"

"Good." But her eyes were bloodshot, and she looked utterly exhausted.

"Is the book you're reading a good one?"

"Intense."

Another one-word answer. What was going on with her? "Why don't you sit down and talk to me while I eat? You know I hate eating alone."

The chair legs scraped over the tile floor, and she sagged into it. "Better?"

I picked up the slice and put it back down. "What is going on with you? Ever since I arrived, you've been talking to me just one word at a time. Does your head hurt? Eyes blurry? Nauseous?"

She opened her mouth, closed it, and then poured a glass of tea and slid it across the table in my direction.

"It's been a long day."

I knew then to change the topic from what her afternoon had been like and talk about the case. "Want to bounce some ideas around about Flora's place?"

Her sable-brown eyes grew wide and I could see the excitement spring to life.

"Do I?" She squirmed in her chair. "Where do you want to start?" Then she looked at me suspiciously. "Are you just trying to pick my brain?"

That was my girl, and her wheels were clicking together. This was going to be fun. "I thought we could collaborate. What's up with the cat door? I don't know if you took a good look, but it was fairly new."

"I found it odd that Flora even had a cat door and then the statue in the yard. Maybe she was thinking of getting a cat?" Her voice trailed off.

"What's on your mind?"

"I was just thinking about the money."

I knew it. She had seen the money under the bed. "What money?"

"Under the bed." She got up and filled the teakettle. "I'm convinced the money is the reason someone killed her, but why? As a librarian, she wouldn't make that kind of money and she has no influence over anything, so bribes are off the table."

It was interesting that she'd use that phrase. "Bribes?"

"Why else would she have that kind of dough?" Lily kept her hands busy as her mind worked out her new theory.

"You don't think this is about a lovers' quarrel gone wrong?" I withdrew my notepad from my shirt pocket. I was old school when it came to writing things down.

"Who was around? I need to think." She leaned against the counter and closed her eyes. "Aunt Mimi was outside, and Nate was with us. Then we had Jill, Marshall, and Teddy." She looked at me. "Are you writing this down?" She waved her hand. "Hold on."

She hurried from the room, and I could hear a closet door open and close and within a minute she was back with a medium-sized blackboard, the kind that stores used to entice people in with the promise of a sale.

"What are you doing?"

She gave me that look like I should already know. "Making a murder board, of course." She propped it in a chair next to the counter and using bright-pink chalk listed the names of everyone at movie night. "Even Nikki and Steve were there, and I remember just before we were going to turn out the lights, I saw Ellis McMahon and Wesley Miles who live at Collins Senior Living Community. I still think it was odd they showed up but..." She even added herself to the list.

Not that I would ever think she had anything to do with it. "Excellent memory. But do you recall if everyone was in the room?"

"Except for Aunt Mimi, who I know wasn't since she found Flora, I'm not one hundred percent sure. Of course, there were people working in the library." She pursed her lips and tapped the chalk on them. "But why the flowers?"

As much as I wanted to sit here and share ideas, my inner cop was reminding me Lily was a civilian and she could get caught in the crossfire of a nasty situation. But I had gotten her wound up.

"Lily, before you spiral too far into the mind of the murderer, I need for you to promise me no more sleuthing on your own."

Her mouth formed a small O. "Milo was with me at Flora's."

"He's a cat, hardly a reliable partner." Her wide smile was not what I wanted to see.

"Not to worry. I'll be careful."

I did not like the overly confident sound in her voice. "Lily. I'm serious. Stay out of the investigation."

She waved a hand around her head and grinned. "You want to waste a resource. My brain?"

"I appreciate your ability to solve all kinds of puzzles, but this one is different and could get you into serious trouble. Promise me, no more investigating on your own."

"That means I can help as long as you're with me or someone else?"

The glint in her eyes made me want to take

her by the shoulders and look her square in the eye to demand she promise she would find another way to utilize her skills. "No. That isn't what I said. You will find another project to focus on. Like that book you've been reading."

Her smile dimmed. "It's not pleasure reading. Aunt Mimi wants me to brush up on our family's history and, at times, it's confusing."

"Now there is a puzzle you can solve." I was relieved to hear that she had something to occupy her mind. "Do you want to talk about it?"

She turned the kettle off and sat down. Milo jumped in her lap and purred loudly as she scratched his ears. "You wouldn't believe me if I told you." The cat batted her hand and she set him down and pointed to the living room.

In the last twenty-four hours, something had changed in her behavior toward Milo. It was as if they were more bonded than ever. Maybe after I caught Flora's killer, I'd need to solve the mystery of Lily and Milo.

Chapter 7
Lily

I didn't enjoy fibbing to Gage, but I had my fingers crossed last night when I implied I wouldn't continue to investigate the murder. Standing in the kitchen, I was studying the murder board when Milo sauntered in.

"I thought you were going to spill the kibble last night and tell your detective that I can talk and that you're a witch. I'll bet that would have sent him running for the dock and the nearest boat he could get on."

I placed his breakfast on the floor and refused to comment on his snark. "I've been thinking about the money and if I could just figure out where it came from, it would solve this murder."

"I'd rather we talk about the book. I was sure you were going to tell Gage it was a book on being a witch. You've never been able to keep anything a secret from him."

"He's one of my best friends, so why would I not tell him?"

Milo tipped his head. "If that's true, then why haven't you ever told him you like, like him?"

"You're right. We need to talk about my witchcraft." I desperately needed to change the subject and get it off Gage. There were some things I might never be ready to tell him. Why would I risk losing his friendship after all these years? "And then, after that, I need to open the shop and figure out a way to casually bump into my first list of suspects."

. . .

Later that morning, I was rereading a section in basic spell casting when Aunt Mimi floated through the door. It was the first time I really noticed she glided around as opposed to how I entered a room which could be less than graceful. Was that part of her witchcraft?

"Good morning, my darling niece."

She was in a fantastic mood and this was promising for me since I had a favor to ask of her. "Hi, Aunt Mimi. What's put the pep in your step?"

"You." She came over and pecked my cheeks as if we were in Europe instead of coastal Maine. She nodded with an approving smile when she saw the book. I had begun to think of the book's name as Dusty, since every page had some layer of dust, causing me to sneeze often.

"I was hoping you were taking your studies seriously. I can see now that you haven't let down the Michaels name."

"Aunt Mimi. It's only been a couple of days. It's not like I knew about this and turned my back on it. But why didn't you give the book to me sooner?"

"It's not about me, Lily. The book knows when a witch is ready. On the day I gave it to you, it appeared on my desk. It's how some of these things work." She lifted her palms skyward. "We just need to be open to what comes next, even at my age."

"What do you mean?" I settled on a tall stool behind the counter. My errand could wait for a bit.

"As a witch, you never stop learning. As your skill grows, so do your needs for different spells. You'll see what I mean in time." She turned the book around so she could see what page I was reading. Nodding with a smile, she asked, "Have you gotten better at finding lost objects?"

I sat up straighter, thinking about Flora's key, which I had found yesterday by focusing. "I used it yesterday, and it went smoothly. I found exactly what I was looking for and pretty quick."

"Excellent. Should we practice a bit before you move on to the next spell, which should be lighting candles? That, too, takes a great deal of focus."

Since I wasn't a huge fan of fire—I had an electric stove after all—I thought that lesson could wait. "Would you be able to watch the shop for me for about an hour? I wanted to run out for something and it won't take long." I didn't dare come across as anxious and hoped my voice sounded easy-breezy.

She gave me a long look, her eyes narrowed. "Are you going to investigate what happened, even though Gage asked you to stay out of it?"

"How did you know?"

"If you want to keep secrets, don't talk in front of Milo, who then turns around and tells my Phoenix. And of course, she tells me. There are zero secrets in the family if your familiar knows."

Now she tells me and why didn't Milo mention that little tidbit? Wait until I saw him later. I needed to know what else he might share with others. A few things needed to be sacred between witch and familiar.

I kissed her soft cheek, and the smell of roses teased my senses. "I won't be long."

I hadn't taken three steps when she commanded, "Wait."

Aunt Mimi took off one of her necklaces that she always wore. It was black tourmaline with amethyst. She placed it around my neck and centered the stones over my heart. "If you insist on running all over town hunting a murderer, the best thing I can do is give you additional protection. Now close your eyes and focus on my words. When I get to the end and say, so shall it be, you'll need to repeat it."

I wasn't sure if crystals would protect me, but if it gave Aunt Mimi comfort, then of course, I'd do or say anything.

She took my hands in hers and said, "Close your eyes."

I did as she asked, suppressing the urge to giggle like a schoolgirl.

"Our mothers who have come before us surround and protect this young witch in search of the truth. I ask for your protection and grace as she is discovering her gifts. Protect Lily from those who may wish to harm her. I ask this with a sincere heart, so shall it be."

I repeated after my aunt, "So shall it be." Was I supposed to feel different somehow? As if a glorious light filled me up like a pitcher under a water faucet?

She kissed me on both cheeks. "Keep a watchful eye."

When I arrived at the library, the yellow crime scene tape was tied around the stairs where Flora had lain. But I was relieved to see no tape on the doors, which in my mind gave me clear approval that I could go inside. The silence was like a cloak around me as I entered the building. Pausing, I slipped off my shoes, realizing I had never been here when I was the only person. I had to admit that right now, it might have been a better idea to not have come alone. What if the killer was inside, searching for clues like I was?

I shivered and pressed forward, determined

to snoop through Flora's desk. Security lights were all I had to guide me on the path since the blinds on the windows were tightly closed. I hesitated. Should I use my cell as a flashlight? But if anyone was close to the windows, they might see it. Better to wait until I really needed it before turning it on.

Every few feet I stopped and listened, closing my eyes to home in on the slightest sound that I may have company. But it was tomb quiet. The irony didn't escape me. Flora would have preferred if the library had been this quiet all the time.

A few more yards and I would be at her desk. I was glad I had slipped my loafers off when I got inside, but the marble floors were freezing. Something clattered in one of the small reference rooms and I became a statue, not daring to breathe or walk to find a different hiding place than behind her desk. I debated. Should I run as fast as humanly possible and get out or stay and find out who else was in here? And there was the matter of looking through the papers.

A slow and steady clicking sound reached my ears. It was soft at first, but getting steadily louder. Without waiting to see who was coming around the corner, I scurried behind the desk, just a few steps away.

The moment I thought I was out of sight, I heard, "Lily, I know you're in here."

Milo? No, it couldn't be. How would he have gotten in? It had to be wishful thinking.

Whoever it was didn't speak again. I was looking to the right when behind me I heard, "Lily, why didn't you answer me?"

I jumped out of my hiding place and whirled around, dropping my loafers in the process. "Milo," I hissed. "How did you get in here?"

"Not with you."

Once again, there was that snark. That was another thing we were going to have to discuss. "I'd appreciate it if when you talk to me, you get that rude tone out of your voice. After all, you're my familiar and I'm the witch."

"That's rich. You'd be a mess if it wasn't for me." He hopped up on Flora's desk and pawed at the papers as if he was looking for something.

"Excuse me." I set him on the floor. "I'll look." Did he even know how to read? Again, all these questions that needed to wait.

"You might want to sit down before you read a couple of those papers." Milo kept a watchful eye on the room.

It was only a suggestion, but it annoyed me. "Why? Am I going to find my name on her list of people to bribe?"

Milo coughed like he had a fur ball. "Don't say I wasn't looking out for you."

As I rifled through the papers, I found the page Milo had referred to. On the top was Mimi Michaels and then most of the people who attended movie night. Next to each name was a dollar amount, and this wasn't a donation for pizza and beer. The amounts were all mid five figures.

My hand shook as I saw my aunt's name had a gold star next to it with an even bigger smiley face. My heart sank. Oh, what was Mimi caught up in?

"Miss Witch, we need to beat feet, or in my case, paws. I just saw a couple of large shadows walk past the window toward the main door."

My mouth went dry. "That's the way I came in."

"Good thing I found a different route. Follow me."

Before I put the papers back, I took a couple of photos on my phone and then ran barefoot after Milo. I was praying whatever way he got in was big enough for a grown woman to get out.

Thank heavens the window had been big enough for me to get out of and when I dropped to the ground, I groaned. I left my shoes near Flora's desk. Milo was waiting for me up ahead and without my loafers. Thinking all the colorful words I wanted to say as I gingerly picked my way down the gravel path, I couldn't help but wonder who was at the library right now and what they would think if they noticed my loafers. Not much I could do unless I could make lost things appear in an entirely different location. Now that is a spell that would really come in handy. I guess I should have studied that old book a little more closely.

When I got home after a busy afternoon, which I worked in my flip-flops, I found my loafers sitting on the back step with a note sticking out. In all honesty, it wasn't much of a note. It was a little funny face and a capital G. One mystery solved. Gage was one of the people who was entering the library while I was snooping. Relief washed over me. Now I didn't need to worry that a killer was after me.

I wanted to broach the subject of my aunt's name on the papers I found in Flora's handwriting. But I had no idea how to do it. I spent the rest of the day working on a spell for turning lights on and off, since I balked at the idea of candles in a bookshop. That sounded like lunacy to me—fire, paper, and me. So not a good combo.

Now that I was home, I turned on my printer

and the photos I had taken with the list of names made an interesting addition to my board. With Mimi Michaels at the top of the list, I refused to think of it as a murder board now.

Shadows crept across the room. All I had done since I got home was stare at the board and pretend to drink a cup of tea. Finally, I decided I needed to clear my head.

"Hey, Nikki. Any chance you'd like to go down to The Clam Bake for dinner? My treat." I got all of that out before she could say no. When she didn't hesitate to say yes, I figured it was the free dinner part that sealed the deal. Nikki was so frugal she probably had the first dollar she got from the tooth fairy. But I loved that about her. She was cautious in all aspects of her life, which some would say was the perfect opposite to me.

"I'll meet you there in a half hour?"

I laughed. "Make it fifteen and I'll spring for dessert."

"I'll see you in ten and I have a tidbit you might find interesting." The smile in her voice lightened my mood, another reason we had been friends forever. She was the yin to my yang, and we had a lot to talk about.

I toyed with the icy mug of draft beer in front of me, unsure where I should start. Witch. Murder. Bribery. Aunt Mimi. And don't forget a talking cat.

"Thanks for meeting me. I was going stir-crazy at home."

She sipped the beer. The foam left a ring on her upper lip. I pointed to it and she dabbed it with a paper napkin from the dispenser.

"I'm happy you did. It seems like we haven't talked for weeks. But I know you've had a lot going on, and I get it. Discovering Mimi over a dead body. Your heartthrob running the case and just turning thirty-eight last week. That's all a lot to handle."

"That's just the half of it." I leaned over the table. She was my best friend and had lived in Pembroke all her life. Maybe she knew about my family's history. "On the day Flora died, I found out I'm a witch."

Nikki's expression didn't change, nor did she laugh like I had expected.

"If that wasn't enough, Milo talks, and he's my familiar. In addition, I believe Flora was killed because she was blackmailing people and Aunt Mimi was on her list." A weight lifted off my shoulders and I felt fifty pounds lighter. Confession was good for the soul.

I took a long drink of my beer and looked up at a smiling Nikki. "Thank the stars you finally know the truth. I've been dying to talk to you about all this. I'm a kitchen witch. What kind of witch are you?"

Chapter 8
Lily

What kind of a witch was I? That was not the comment I had been expecting. Or to learn that Nikki was a witch too. "You're not shocked, scared, or surprised in the least?"

She laughed. "Are you kidding? I've always felt that you had magic in you, but for some reason it was stuck in idle and now we can get you up to speed." She snapped her fingers and I swear it wasn't possible, but her smile got even bigger. "Does Gage know?"

"Other than Aunt Mimi, Nate, and Milo, you're the only person who knows."

"You haven't called your mom yet?"

I shook my head. "I've been a little busy trying to solve this mystery and now that"—I looked around the huge empty room and lowered my voice—"now that Aunt Mimi is on the top of the suspect list, that will be my sole focus until the case is solved."

Nikki clapped her hands together like we were on a fun scavenger hunt. "What can I do to help?"

I waved my hand in the air to slow the roll she was starting to get on. "Do you have a familiar?"

"All witches do, silly. I have Murphy."

"But he's a golden retriever." Now I was totally confused. Weren't cats always the familiar? At least that is how it was in books and movies.

"A familiar can be any creature that you bond with or who is a part of your legacy. Just as Milo was a legacy for you."

Her sweet smile did nothing to soothe my confusion. "How did you know about Milo?"

"One look and any witch would know. You two are a good pair."

"How long have you been a witch?"

She twirled a lock of hair around her finger. "Since I started baking wedding cakes. It's part of my craft to create delicious cakes for brides and grooms."

"But you're a newspaper reporter. Being a kitchen witch doesn't jibe." My head was aching again, and all I wanted to do was clear all thoughts that didn't have to do with the murder. Aunt Mimi's freedom might just depend on it.

"The two don't need to be a perfect blend of your job and your talent."

We stopped talking when the seafood pupu platter was delivered along with sides of coleslaw and rolls. After the teenage girl left us and before Nikki could start eating, I needed to know what she had meant when we talked earlier. That she had a tidbit of intel.

She had a fried clam dripping in tartar sauce

poised to go into her mouth when I stopped her by asking, "What was that tidbit you teased earlier?"

Without missing a beat, she popped it in and closed her eyes. "This is so good," she mumbled with a full mouth. "You gotta try one."

There would be time for savoring fried food as soon as I knew what she knew.

When Nikki opened her eyes, she gave a half laugh. "Guess you'll eat after I spill the beans, huh?"

"Something like that."

"I was going into Robin's Café right before lunch. Jill, Marshall, and Teddy were sitting near the door. It looked like they'd been there a while since coffee cups were empty and napkins and crumbs were littering the table."

Nikki needed to get to the point. But details were important, so I didn't rush her story and she had a good idea even if her puzzling skills weren't quite as good as mine. In my head that sounded better than it would have come out, so I pushed that thought aside.

"When I walked by, they were talking about Flora's murder and about scads of money that were unaccounted for. I got the impression Jill was about to ask a question until she saw me lingering by the newspaper rack."

"I take it they changed the subject." I was elated and disappointed at the same time. The evidence was there that the three of them knew about the money. One of them must be the killer, or could it be they planned and executed it together?

Nikki jabbed a finger at my forehead. "Don't strain your brain even though it's in high gear. But even Robin was talking about Flora's stash of money to that Wesley guy."

"So that wasn't a secret, but it's still the motive. I'm sure of it." I dipped a fish nugget into the creamy horseradish sauce and ate it without tasting. "This wasn't tied to the library. So did it have to do with the work she did on the town council?"

"There's a company that wants to tear down a bunch of nice older homes for a luxury spa. Nothing we'd want here, but an LLC submitted paperwork even on the semi-historical sites and it would change the look of Pembroke forever."

"You're right, so that is a nonissue. Then why were the three most unlikely people in this town riding together the night of the murder and today meeting for coffee, and in a public café?" The more I thought about it, odd didn't begin to cover it. I couldn't put my finger on what was bugging me other than I didn't know they were even friends.

"Why do you think your aunt is on the top of that list you saw?" Licking ketchup from the tips of her fingers, Nikki's half of the platter was almost empty. Where did she hide it? She didn't have an extra curve on her frame.

That was a good question. And one I didn't have an answer for. "As soon as I discover that, I'll let you know. I'm going to talk with Aunt Mimi tomorrow, but first we're going to take a drive if you're up for a little adventure."

Nikki narrowed her eyes and turned her

head to the right and left. "What are you thinking?"

With the restaurant nearly empty, I said, "Just a little after-dinner drive. Nothing too exciting." I leaned forward and caught the pendant from my protection necklace. It grew warm under my fingers. "Are you in?"

She nodded, and her eyes sparkled with mischief. "But I'll drive so you can look. Where to first?"

"We'll drive out past Marshall's farm first since he's the farthest out of town and then cruise past Jill's before the final destination, Teddy's."

She wiggled her fingers. "I'll wash up and meet you out front."

I signaled for the check and left her a healthy tip. I remembered what it was like on a slow night waiting tables. They appreciated every dollar. Then I hurried to meet Nikki in the lobby. This was going to be exciting.

. . .

Driving by Marshall and Jill's home was dull. Both houses were dark, and Jill's car wasn't in her driveway. Her outside lights were on, which led me to believe she had gone out for a bit and expected to be home after dark. Marshall's was just as dark. Maybe he was working late. Being a farmer, that didn't make much sense, but I guessed there would be nights he got hung up working on equipment. But Jill not being home was curious. There were no events downtown that I knew of.

As we turned down the street where Teddy lived, I said, "When you drive past Teddy's place, go slow."

Nikki slowed the car to little more than a crawl. I walked faster than she was driving, but it gave me the opportunity to scope things out. I grabbed her arm. "Look. In the front window." Why they hadn't pulled the drapes was beyond me, but from the street I could see Marshall, Jill, and Teddy sitting around the dining room table, with a fourth person I had never seen before. My heart kicked up. This was just what I had been hoping for—finding them together again. There was no doubt they had something to do with Flora's death.

I pointed to a turnout next to the road. More than likely, a place where a delivery or mail truck might pull off. "Park over there and turn the car off." I looked back over my shoulder at the house. "I need to get a closer look and maybe with any luck Teddy will have a window open so I can hear what they're talking about."

"That's not a good idea, Lily. Maybe we should call Gage."

I couldn't believe my ears. The newspaper reporter wanted to kill the lead of a potential story by calling the local cops. I didn't think so.

"You can stay in the car. Keep an eye on me and if I whistle, be prepared to take off as soon as I get back to the car." I pushed open the passenger door and closed it softly. No sense in alerting anyone about me being here. Before I got around the back of the car, Nikki was closing her door.

"I'm going with you." She linked her arm

through mine while we crossed the street and then let me take the lead. Not that I knew what I was going to do next, but I swallowed the butterflies that raced in my throat and dropped to the ground to crawl like a crab along the front of the house.

If I had been thinking clearly, I would have realized this would look suspicious if someone drove by. I motioned for Nikki to do the same, but she didn't get on her knees. She just squatted down and pointed to her pale-green capris. I smiled. There was no way she would get grass and dirt stains on her clothes unless it was a dire emergency.

As I made my way along the ground, I moved with care so as not to snap a twig or make any kind of sound. When I got to where I thought the dining room was closest, I held up a hand to Nikki, indicating I was going to stop moving, but she must not have seen me as she ran into my backside and sent me sprawling. So much for not making any noise. They had to have heard that crash.

I held my breath and waited, sensing my partner in crime was doing the same. I was about ready to give up and signal we should go back to the car when the sound of a man's voice caught my attention. Could it be Marshall?

"I'd like to thank the person who did Flora in. We sure caught a break and it saved us a ton of money. I for one was tired of making my monthly contributions to the Flora Gray retirement fund."

A female voice was next, and it could only be Jill. "I wish there was a way for the cops to give us back what we paid her, but short of telling them what was going on and hoping for the best, that just will not happen."

Just when I thought we were really getting somewhere, I heard Nikki sneeze softly. She poked at my leg and whispered, "We have to go. I'm allergic to something."

Even though she whispered, it sounded like shouting to me since the last thing we needed was to be caught eavesdropping outside Teddy's house. I put a finger across my lips and held it up, indicating one more minute.

That's when I heard her sneeze building. Before we had a chance to back up and move away from the front of the house, she let out a large *achoo*!

Teddy yelled from inside the house. I grabbed Nikki's hand and we ran as fast as we could. There was no way we'd get back to her car and away before being seen, so I pulled her in the direction of the parallel street. Once we got around the corner, we'd be able to pretend like we were just out walking if anyone caught us.

My pendant was swinging wildly, and I grabbed it so it wouldn't smack me in the face as I ran. Its warmth calmed me and I slowed. I just knew we were safe. I turned. No one was chasing us either.

"Nikki. Slow down. We're good." With deep heaving breaths, I attempted to get enough oxygen so my words didn't come out like each one was going to be my last. The choppy sentences would have to suffice for good English.

Her stride shortened, and she grinned at me. "That was fun, but next time I'll need to take allergy meds before we go out snooping."

With a cocked brow, I said, "I prefer to think of it as following the clues. And I'm not sure what you heard, but one of them is responsible. I just know it."

I finally arrived home after dark and I hadn't left any lights on when I went to dinner. My bad. I put the car in the garage and was ready to walk through the laundry room when I stopped. It looked as if a mini tornado had whirled through my dirty clothes. What the heck had happened? My next thought was for Milo. Whatever had gone on here, he'd better be safe.

Without giving it another thought, I flicked on the lights as I stormed through the house. "Milo. Where are you?"

I could hear him calling to me, but his voice was muffled. Where the heck was he? I called again and his kitty voice was a little louder as I walked into my office. This room had gotten the worst of it and they had wiped my murder board clean. A scratching on the closet door drew my attention, and I pulled it open and dropped to the floor to scoop up my friend.

"Milo, are you alright?" I kissed the top of his soft head and rubbed his ears.

"What took you so long to get home?" He smacked my arm with his claws and hopped onto my desk. "I've been trying to reach you." He looked at the book in my arms. "Let me guess. You haven't finished the book yet." He hung his head and shook it.

I could tell he was disappointed, but honesty was my only choice. "I'm still working on lighting candles. But I seem to have the location spell down pat." I forced a grin to my lips, but he wasn't having any of it.

"Read. The. Book." He jumped down. "Call Gage and don't talk to me until you've finished reading. Oh, and Mimi dropped it off. It's in the kitchen."

He stalked out of the room and I was

tempted to just clean up my house, but Milo was right. Gage needed to see this for himself. Especially since my murder board had been wiped clean.

On the second ring, he answered. "Um, hi, Gage. Any chance you can swing by? I think someone knows I'm investigating Flora's murder."

Chapter 9
Gage

By the time I arrived at Lily's house, my heart was thundering and my lungs were on fire as if I ran five miles at top speed. Cop instinct said she was in danger and at the moment, I was helpless to protect her. All because she had tried to solve the crime. What had I been thinking, encouraging her? Even if her mind was the best I had ever encountered when it came to solving puzzles. I tried to open the door, but it was locked.

"Lily!" I rapped on the glass so hard it rattled in the frame.

The door opened and she threw her arms around my neck. I held her tight. "I got here as fast as I could."

She hadn't released me yet. Her voice was muffled against my chest. "They locked Milo in the closet."

"They didn't hurt him, did they?"

"No. But it's mean." She sniffled.

There was a part of me that hoped the incident tonight would convince her to stop poking around. "He's alright, and that's all that matters, right?" I could feel her head nod against my chest. "Why don't we go inside and I can look around."

She slowly loosened her grip on me and took a tiny step back. "The house is a mess."

I gave her a smile. "It's okay. I'll help you clean up after I look around."

I took her hand as we walked into the house, and it was worse than I had imagined. Every cabinet door and drawer was open in the kitchen. Some food containers with dried pasta, crackers, and coffee had been opened and scattered on the floor. Was this in part to make a mess because they could or because she might have hid something important in a random box? I noticed the laundry room and the scattered clothes. I was trying to remain cool and professional, but it was hard. This was Lily, not just an average person from the community.

"The office got the worst of it."

Her voice was soft, and I had to strain to hear what she said. I gave her hand a squeeze. Hopefully, it reassured her.

"Is there anything missing?"

I thought it would be hard to tell with such a mess, but Lily shook her head. "No. Well, yes, my murder board was erased and with it, my notes of what I've discovered so far."

My gaze was sharp as I looked at her. "Had you added much since I was here?"

"Just some random thoughts, nothing major." She tapped her temple. "But I've got it up here and I have news to share with you, too."

"Oh, Lily. Only you could still be focused on my investigation while we're looking at your crime scene." I shuddered as those words came out of my mouth. "You *have* to stop. This was a warning that someone could get into your house when you aren't home."

"I guess I need to lock my doors."

My steps came to a halt. "Your doors were unlocked?"

With eyes wide and innocent, she said, "Of course. We live in a small sleepy town. Nothing bad ever happens here."

I swept the room with a wide-armed gesture. "This is nothing?" How was I going to get through to her? Whoever did this was sending her a strong warning.

She lifted her shoulder and gave me a sheepish smile. "It means I'm on the right track." She frowned. "But if I only knew what I had discovered and what was making the murderer nervous." Her eyes got bright. "Do you think it could be the same person who left the box?"

"And you just said a critical word—murderer." I pulled her to my chest and held her there, more for my comfort than hers. "And I'm going to surmise it's the same person."

"I'll be more careful. I promise, Gage." She wriggled from my arms and approached her tent chalkboard. "Is it okay if I set this back up?"

"I need pictures for my report, so give me a few minutes." I withdrew my cell and took pictures of her office. Before I walked around the rest of the house, I hovered in the doorway, watching her, and my heart constricted. "Lily?"

She was picking up books from the floor and setting them in her bookcases, which lined two walls in her office.

She turned and smiled at me. "I can call out for pizza if you want to stay. I ate with Nikki earlier, but all of this has made me hungry."

"I could eat a slice." I pulled out my phone and called in Lily's favorite—the supreme with extra cheese—and I added an order of mozzarella sticks just in case she was really feeling the stress.

· · ·

We were sitting in the living room with the open pizza box on the coffee table and mugs of ice-cold beer in hand. "Now that I'm stuffed, why don't you tell me what you and Nikki were up to earlier, since I'm sure this was somehow related." I half turned on the couch so I could see every facial expression on Lily's face. The truth was always in her tells.

She put her mug aside and her eyes danced with excitement. Whatever she was about to say would not make me happy or comfortable.

"We went to dinner at The Clam Bake and over a bunch of fried food, we were talking about the case. You know what she might have seen at the library and those notes I saw there."

A lead weight hit the bottom of my gut. What exactly had she seen?

She pulled out her cell phone and showed me photos of the pages she had found. It was the list of numbers and names.

"You shouldn't have taken pictures. This might be what the person was looking for."

She grinned. "That's why I'm smarter than

the average bear." She scrolled through a couple more and her smile fell. "I was really worried when I saw Aunt Mimi's name was first on the list. So that either means she's already given Flora money or she was next on the list of targets."

"And how did you come to that conclusion?"

She looked at me like I had four heads. "Oodles of money in her house for starters and the biggest tidbit I learned tonight was after Nikki and I went for a drive past Marshall's, Jill's, and then Teddy's houses. I discovered them sitting around Teddy's table with someone I didn't recognize."

I heard the triumphant ah-ha in her voice like it was conclusive evidence of wrongdoing on their part. "And what were they doing?"

"That's just it. They were talking about Flora and how it was a good thing she was dead before they had to make, and I quote, 'more contributions to the Flora Gray retirement fund.'"

I had to admit that did sound suspicious, but it was hardly evidence that one of them killed her. I was about to point that out when it occurred to me there was a part of her story she hadn't mentioned.

"How did you hear this conversation?"

"I crawled along the foundation and was crouched under the dining room window. That is until Nikki sneezed and we had to take off running."

I smacked my beer on the table, not caring. The liquid sloshed on the wood. "You did what?"

"How else was I supposed to eavesdrop on the suspects?"

I got up and paced the room. "You're not a police officer and this is not your job. When you get a cockamamie idea like that again, you call me first. Stay away from these people. They could be dangerous."

"Nothing happened. They didn't even see us. Besides, there's no way any of them could have done this. When we drove by to come home, they were still sitting around the table."

I leaned against the fireplace, taking deep

calming breaths. At least I was hoping they'd calm me. "Did you come straight home?"

She chewed on her bottom lip. "Well, no. We left my car at the restaurant, so we went back to pick it up, and then I stopped at the pet store to get Milo some treats."

"So from the time you left Teddy's place, how long before you got home?" Based on my rough estimate, one of them had plenty of time, but it would be better if she figured it out and by the way her eyes grew as round as saucers and her mouth gaped open, she just did.

"I just remembered something important."

"About how long before you got home?"

She waved her hands as if cutting me off mid-sentence. "On the ground at the library. There was a butterscotch wrapper, right near Flora."

"Okay, that could have come from any-where." I wanted to get the conversation back to tonight.

"No, let me explain. That night, there was a bowl of hard candies on a table and Flora made a rude comment about having to clean up the wrappers. What if whoever brought those candies had something to do with her death? It would make sense."

"Lots of people eat hard candy. It's inconsequential to the case."

"I'm adding it to my murder board, anyway. I think if we find out who threw that one to the ground that might just be our guy."

"Can we get back to tonight now?" I wanted to impress upon her that her actions had serious implications.

"Forty-five minutes, more or less." She scooped up the leftovers and hurried into the kitchen, as if trying to end the conversation.

I followed her. "That was more than enough time to leave Teddy's, come here, mess up the house, and get out before you got home."

"Pretty bold." Lily handed me the leftover pizza wrapped in foil.

"Is this your way of asking me to leave?" I held up the packet. "I'm going to sit outside the house for a while just in case someone comes back, but please do me a favor and don't go off to check out any more ideas tonight."

She kissed my cheek, and the clean scent of sunshine filled my senses. "I have some reading to do tonight, so I promise I'll be here, and if I get any fresh ideas, I'll call you first." She held up her pinky and looped hers with mine. "I promise."

"Good." I brushed her hair back from her eyes and wanted so much to lean in and kiss her, but I would never put our friendship in jeopardy. "I'll talk to you tomorrow."

A flicker of what might have been disappointment flared in her eyes, but it was gone so fast it might have been my imagination. I tore my eyes away and walked to the door before I changed my mind and did the exact opposite of what my heart told me to do. "Good night, Lily." I jiggled the doorknob. "Lock up from now on."

"Thanks for coming over and not to worry. Until you catch this person, my doors will be locked."

It was a start, so for now I'd let it go. "Talk in the morning?"

She smiled with her hand on the doorjamb. "Come by the shop and I'll have coffee and pastries, say nine thirty?"

"It's a date." I cringed. That was not the right thing to say, but it was out there and I was not about to make it more awkward. I walked out and said good night one more time, waiting for the door to close after me.

Sitting in my car, I could see Lily walking around her living room, holding an open book and she seemed to be talking to someone. After a time, Milo appeared on the back of the chair and I peered closer. What was she doing? Having a conversation with her cat? This situation must have affected her more than I realized.

Chapter 10
Lily

I looked out through the blinds and saw Gage's car was gone. He had hung around for about an hour, as far as I could tell. I looked at Milo perched on the back of a chair. "Gage took off."

He swished his tail and coughed like he was trying to get up a hairball. "About time. We have work to do."

I touched the pendant that hung around my neck. "Do you think it's possible the reason Nikki and I didn't get caught tonight was the protection necklace from Aunt Mimi?" Once again, it grew warm under my touch and I couldn't help but wonder why.

"More importantly. What do you think?"

I didn't like it when anyone turned a question back on me and it irritated me that my cat was doing it now. But to stop the ping-pong conversation, I said, "Yes. It gets warm from time to time and I think that's when it's stronger."

He gave a nod. "Your instincts are starting to kick in. That's good." With a paw, he turned the page of the book. "Let's get back to candles. It might not seem like an important skill, but it's a basic building block for other things you'll need to learn."

"Can't I do something else, like to learn to fly? Now that would come in handy." My attempt to lighten the mood fell flat.

"You are nowhere near ready to fly. That might not be for years to come."

"Milo, I was joking."

If a cat could give a haughty look, that's how Milo glared at me and I stood there not moving. "I'll be able to fly? Like on a broom?"

"Back to the book." He flicked his tail one last time and left me staring after him. This was going to be a lot of education that I wasn't sure I could handle. My only comfort was my best friend also being a witch. Maybe she could give me pointers.

When I dragged myself into the bookshop the next morning, seeing the sign for The Cozy Nook Bookshop brightened my mood. I was tired and annoyed with myself. I kept going over and over who might have trashed my home and how I was going to talk to the suspects on my list. Except for Aunt Mimi; I didn't know how to approach her. What I needed was a do-over movie night. I thought about calling Meredith at the library. She was, or had been, Flora's assistant for years and now it seemed she would be in charge. With any luck, the same space would be available. Then I'd have a reason to call everyone who had been there to let them know we would be watching the movie.

While I waited for Gage to arrive, I dialed the library and waited for Meredith to answer. I also shot a quick text to Nikki, asking if she could grab coffee and something sweet from the pastry shop. She answered with a thumbs-up emoji.

"Hello. Pembroke Library, this is Meredith." Her breathy voice was more rushed than I remembered.

"Hi, Meredith, it's Lily Michaels." I paused, giving her a moment to switch gears as I'm sure her head was in a stack of books.

"Lily, this is a surprise. What can I do for you?"

This sounded promising. Not at all like talking to Flora when she snapped every time I called to set up an event. "I was hoping we could reschedule movie night in the next couple of days. The group was really looking forward to seeing *Death on the Nile* and it's such a good movie. I have to admit I am looking forward to it, too."

The line was silent, and I wondered if we had been disconnected. Finally, she said, "The police have given us permission to reopen, so I don't see why not. The detective, Gage Erikson, didn't put any restrictions on us, so I'm sure it would be just fine. When did you want to use the room?"

I didn't expect her to agree so quickly, so I had to think fast. "How about Monday night?" That would give me four days to contact everyone and it was our usual movie night, which might make it easier to get everyone to come. I was pretty pleased with my ability to think on my feet. And having all the suspects under one roof, so to speak, was sure to crack this case wide open.

"I'll mark you down and just check in with me when you arrive."

"Thank you, Meredith, and I wanted to ask, how are you doing?"

"I'm fine." Her voice did sound light and breezy. "You should stop by the library to make sure the room is set up the way you need it. No one has been in there since, you know, since Monday."

"Did we leave it a mess? I know Flora asked us to clean up when we were done, but I think once Aunt Mimi screamed, we all just forgot."

"Don't worry about that. I'm not. I just want everything to be perfect for your movie buffs."

This was a refreshing change. "Thank you so much, Meredith. I'll stop by later today if that's okay with you."

"We're open until six tonight."

Once again, I was struck by how relaxed she sounded. Working for Flora must have been very difficult. I made a note on the pad next to my cash register to bring her a cupcake or something, just to show my appreciation.

We said our goodbyes, and I set the phone aside as Nikki rushed in carrying a pastry box and a tray with three coffees. I handed her a twenty for doing the pickup.

"I have news. We're going to have movie night on Monday. So, you and Steve have to come. I'm hoping to get the same group there who was around the night Flora died."

Her brow furrowed, and she crossed her

arms over her body. "Do you think that's a good idea? One of those people might be the person who killed Flora."

"That's what I'm counting on. But don't worry, I'm going to make sure Gage comes too as backup."

The door opened as if on cue, and the handsome detective walked in. "Did I hear someone say they needed backup?" He looked from Nikki to me.

I couldn't hold back a grin. "You did. And before you say no, hear me out. I have a great idea, but I need you to agree."

Nikki handed him a cup of coffee. "You're going to need this and you might even want to sit down."

He took the cup and smiled his thanks before turning to me. "I'm not going to like this, am I?"

"You should. I'm not breaking my promise, and I'm telling you what I'm doing."

He settled in one of the wingback chairs and crossed one foot over his knee. "I'm listening."

I picked up the box heavy with what I was

sure was to-die-for treats and my coffee so I could sweeten Gage up before I launched into my plan. "Croissant."

He took one and I passed the box to Nikki, who had sat down on another chair close by. I was sure she didn't want to miss the fireworks that were about to ensue. She shook her head and sipped her coffee. I had to wonder if this might be one of the secrets to her figure. Refocusing, I gave Gage a smile.

"I was thinking about everything that happened the night that Flora was killed, and I keep coming up empty. Other than what we know, she had been blackmailing people, for heaven only knows what, which explains the money. Was that a motive for murder? Possibly." I paused for dramatic effect and to see if Gage would interject something here about the case that I might not know, but since he didn't, I continued with my train of thought.

"What better way than to get everyone together who was there that night and we can watch the film. Maybe someone will slip up and mention something to point the finger at the real culprit."

Now Gage leaned forward and set the croissant on a paper napkin on the table. "How do you think that might happen?"

"People see things that at the time seem unimportant or even normal. What if someone at movie night witnessed someone leaving or coming in late? And then they say something like, where did you go the other night? Or I didn't see you come in or leave. Things like that." I wasn't sure if Gage was pleased with my idea or if he was about to shut me down. I glanced at Nikki and she gave me a wink, as if I was on the right track.

He sipped his coffee but didn't speak for what seemed like *forever*. I wanted to poke him, but it was his process to think about the angles and come to his own conclusion. Even though I was certain this was a fantastic idea.

While he was deep in thought, a woman came in. I got up to help her find the latest in a romance series I knew she liked. After I checked her out, I returned to the seating area and once again waited. Nikki glanced at her watch as if she had some place she needed to be. But if she wanted to say she was working on this article, she was completely justified in hanging out as long as necessary.

Finally, Gage gave me a nod. "It might work, but only with several conditions."

I wanted to high-five Nikki and Gage, but thought he might frown on that and rescind his readiness to help.

"You don't interrogate anyone during movie night. Your normal chatter is just fine." He gave me a smile, knowing that I would find his use of the word *chatter* to be a touch annoying, but I rolled with it, anyway.

"Agreed. What else?" I was feeling confident this was going to work out with him making an arrest and we could finally watch the movie. "When you spread the word, all you do is mention the movie, nothing about all the suspects gathering."

"I can live with that, but can I tell Aunt Mimi what I'm doing?"

He shook his head. "No. She's still a suspect."

My mouth dropped open. "Are you kidding? You've known her your entire life. How can you say she's a suspect?"

He gave me a long look, as if I should know the answer. But he explained anyway. "You found her standing over the body and her name is on a key piece of evidence. Until there is proof that she shouldn't be considered, she's a suspect. To be honest, the only reason you're not is everyone I spoke to concurred you were in the room when Mimi screamed."

I plastered my hand on my chest. "You would have considered me too? But we're like best friends." I glanced at Nikki and followed up with, "No offense."

She smiled, and I turned back to Gage. "Would you think Nikki is capable too?"

He gave me an indulgent smile, which annoyed me. I clasped my protection pendant, but it was cool to the touch. There was no danger here other than a good teasing.

"Everyone is on my list until I can take them off. For the record, you and Nikki are both off my list." He grinned.

I was at a loss for words and wasn't sure how to even continue this conversation. Nikki said, "So, who are still your most likely suspects?"

He looked at the door as if expecting someone to walk in at any second. "I shouldn't even answer that question. Suffice it to say anyone who had a number next to their name on Flora's list is being closely looked at."

Nikki looked at me. "I never saw it."

I held up a finger, asking her to wait, and I retrieved my phone. "I have photos."

She grinned. "Of course you do." As she scrolled through the pictures, she groaned. "One third of the town is on this list. How are you going to narrow it down?"

Gage held out his hand for the phone, and he looked at the pictures, too. "I've cross-referenced people who were at movie night or don't have a clear alibi for that time of day to everyone on this list. I'll continue to refine it, but overall, I'm down to about six strong possibilities."

Who was he referring to as the six? I only had four on my list—three if you didn't count my aunt. "Who are they?"

He waved a finger back and forth and I swear he would have said *tsk tsk*, if he could have gotten away with it, but he would have never lived that down with me or Nikki.

"You know four and leave it at that."

I knew that set of his jawline and he would not give me any additional details. At least not today. "I have already called the library and Meredith said using the room would be no problem."

"When do you plan on getting the word out?" Nikki chimed in. "I can help if you want. Get something in the paper."

Under normal circumstances, putting an announcement in the paper was a great way to drum up attendees, but for this event, I really only wanted the people who had been there orig-inally. "Thanks, Nikki, but not this time."

Gage checked his watch and got up. "I have to take off, but I'll call you later." His fingertips grazed my shoulder. "Stay out of trouble today." He gave Nikki a stern look. "That goes for you too."

"Yes, Detective." She flashed him a demure smile. There was no way to know the minute he walked out the door we would plan our next foray into investigating.

I told him we'd talk later and waited for the door to close firmly behind him. Then I looked at Nikki.

"The next thing on our list is to talk to my aunt and find out why she was on the blackmail list. It might help us to determine what Flora was doing and why. If it was blackmail, we need to get solid proof so that Gage will have something to look into."

She cast a worried look in the direction where Gage had walked down the street. "Do you think he's going to get mad at us?"

I cocked a brow. "Do you know of a spell to find out the future?"

"No, and we're not going to go looking for one either. Besides, you have enough to learn."

I slumped back into the chair. "Why does everyone keep telling me that? I have the location spell down pat and I'm working on lighting candles. What comes after that?"

Nikki leaned forward and patted my knee. "It's different for every witch. But don't worry, your book will lead the way."

"That's what Milo said too." I didn't want to get off this chair and do any work. When I closed my eyes, I thought of Aunt Mimi. I really needed to talk to her and not just about my book, but also to find out why her name was on Flora's list.

Nikki prodded my foot with hers. "Don't look now, but your aunt is coming across the street and she's making a beeline for the shop."

I sat up and looked at the door. Aunt Mimi came in like a hurricane, beaming with pride. The moment she saw me, she said, "What's so urgent that I had to get here in such a hurry?"

This was confusing. "Aunt Mimi, what are you talking about?"

"Didn't you use the summoning spell to call me?"

I tipped my head to the side and thought about what I had read in the book last night. Now that she mentioned it, I had fallen asleep while reading, having been frustrated I couldn't get the candles to light. Maybe my subconscious absorbed more than my conscious while holding the book.

"If I did, I'm sorry, Aunt Mimi. I was reading it last night, but I didn't know I could actually make it work. Especially since the whole fire thing is a failure."

She placed her handbag on the coffee table and peeked inside the box. "Nonsense. You'll get it. Just give it more time. But now, tell me why you needed to see me in such a hurry, and I'll enjoy this luscious-looking éclair." She sat down and licked the extra icing from her fingertips. "And just FYI, you did the summoning spell perfectly. I knew exactly where you were and how quickly you needed to see me. Well done."

I sat up straighter, knowing that at least I would not be a total washout as a witch. "Now, Aunt Mimi, please tell us, and this is off the record for Nikki too. Why was your name on a list that Flora had with an amount of fifty thousand dollars next to it?"

Aunt Mimi choked and sputtered. "How did you find out about that?"

I was getting good at this sleuthing business. I just smiled and said, "I asked you first."

Chapter 11
Lily

Aunt Mimi set her éclair on a plate on the table. "I'm not sure how she comes across any of her information, but she learned something very private about me and Nate and it's not something we want to share right now."

"What did she know and did she tell you to pay her in order to keep her mouth shut?"

"Not exactly. At the library on movie night, she told me to meet her outside but to give her ten minutes and then follow. That way, if anyone saw us together, they wouldn't ask questions.

Nate wanted to go with me, but I told him I would be fine and I wouldn't be gone long. Heck, how long could it take to tell someone you weren't going to give them a red cent?"

"Aunt Mimi, what could she have on you that Flora would believe you'd be willing to pay to keep her quiet?"

"That is none of your business." Her voice was firm and there was no changing her mind. She wiped her fingers daintily on her napkin and got up from the chair. Her face was crimson, and she clutched her handbag as if hanging on for dear life. "People have a right to keep some things in their life private until they are ready to share." She stormed out the door without a backward glance and it slammed shut behind her with a resounding *thud*.

Nikki looked at me and judging by the way her face was scrunched up, she didn't have a clue what went on here either.

"From what Aunt Mimi just said, that gives her a stronger motive than before that she killed her. Not only was Flora intent on extracting money from her and Nate, but she was outside at almost the same time as Flora's murder. If Gage knew any of this, he'd have to arrest my aunt."

Nikki said, "Keep your voice down. You never know who could be outside listening."

I knew she was thinking about our adventure last night and nodded. "Are you up for an adventure tonight?"

Her eyes sparkled with mischief and excitement. "Just try to leave me behind." It was more apparent than ever that we needed to talk with the three musketeers before Monday night if there was any hope of an arrest and making sure it wasn't Aunt Mimi in handcuffs.

The rest of the day the shop was quiet. I went back to the candle spell but no matter how hard I tried, I ended up spitting on the wick. The total opposite of what I was supposed to do. I slammed the book shut and jumped when I heard a gravelly voice speak.

"Frustrated?"

I was so intent on trying to learn the spell that I didn't hear Milo come in. The good news, he was still speaking to me, so I was doing something right.

"Milo, I'm a failure as a witch." I propped my elbows on the book and hoped I didn't look as down as I felt.

"That's not what I hear. Word has it you did a summoning spell, which is very good and as far as lighting candles or even turning on lights, your strengths might lie in other areas. But don't give up."

"I can find things that are missing and I can summon my aunt. Neither of these will help me solve Flora's murder to save my aunt."

"Gage will take care of that; have some faith in him."

"I do, but from what Mimi just told me, once he finds out why she was outside, he'll probably have to arrest her." I could feel the tears welling up in my eyes as my heart constricted so tight it ached. Aunt Mimi was a second mom to me, and I just couldn't bear the thought of anything happening to her. Besides, Mom would be ticked as all get out if I let that happen.

"The best way to help Mimi is to study the book and learn all you can. At some point, a little magic might be helpful."

I studied Milo carefully. Not that a cat could really have a tell, but just in case. His nose twitched but it could be the dust from the book. It was still throwing off clouds from different pages. "Are you clairvoyant?"

"Really, you think a mere cat will be given such an awesome power?"

I noticed he wasn't answering my question. Maybe the cat had a sixth sense besides nine lives. As if he were a naughty child, I shook my finger at him. "I hope you're being honest, for both our sakes. I'm pretty sure being a witch can get me into a bit of trouble."

"And that's why you have me to keep you on the straight as a broomstick path."

I laughed at his attempt at humor. I didn't even know if brooms were straight. Did you just use the one from the pantry closet or was there something special? And he had never been up-front about that. Did we fly?

Not for lack of me trying, Milo wouldn't budge from practicing the candle spell yet again. When he wasn't looking, I texted Nikki to see if she wanted to be my backup when I went to see Jill Dilly. It wouldn't really hurt to hear what she might have seen on movie night. After she sent back yes with an exclamation point, I spent some time concentrating on the beeswax candle in front of me. Milo had suggested I run down to Bee Bee's Boutique for a candle that was short, fat, and most definitely beeswax. He thought if I was practicing on something from nature, it would make it easier. Who was I to second-guess my cat?

I sat at the counter on a stool with the candle in front of me. I adjusted the wick so it was standing straight up. In my mind, I could see a flicker of flame appear. If I didn't figure this out soon, I was moving on and just buying a lot of matches. Shutting my eyes, I kept that mental picture in the forefront. I pursed my lips and more gently than a light summer breeze, I blew across the wick to the slow count of one, two. I opened my eyes and there was a wisp of smoke fluttering up from the wick.

"Milo, look."

He was watching the wisp too. "Again, just like the last time. Only count to three."

I took a deep breath and I could feel my body relax into the moment. This would be something I conquered today. I closed my eyes again and with barely an exhale, I blew over the wick. Before I got to the count of three, I opened them just in time to see the wick catch into a steady flame. I couldn't believe it. I had done it!

He tapped his paw on my palm after I held up my hand to high-five him. I now had completed two, possibly three, if I could count the summoning spell. I doused the candle so that I could do it again. This time it had to be easier, and I kept my eyes open but still focused. I hadn't even gotten to two when it flickered to life. I wanted to jump up and tell everyone I knew I had lit a candle with just a breath and determination. But the only people I could tell were Nikki and Aunt Mimi.

I didn't hesitate. Even if she was upset with me earlier, I knew she'd want to hear this good news. When she didn't answer, I left her a message to call me when she had a minute. Milo was sitting next to the closed book.

"Are you ready for the next lesson?"

The third spell I had read about was summoning. Since it had worked earlier in the day from what my aunt said, maybe I should try it and see what might happen. I hadn't retained the words, so instead I improvised. "Ala kazoo, ala kazam, I need Aunt Mimi, right where I am."

Milo hissed. "What was that?"

I shrugged my shoulders. "I thought I'd go off book. Just to see if it worked." I watched the door as if my aunt would magically appear. I had to chuckle to myself since Milo would never have found the humor in my thoughts.

"I guess it didn't work." Flipping open the

cover on the book, it surprised me to realize I was disappointed. My talent must have to follow instructions precisely to work. Before I got back to the work of a witch, I decided on a hot beverage. It was going to be a long couple of hours before Nikki would be free.

"I need a break. I'm making a pot of tea. Would you like something too? A catnip ball, saucer of kitty milk?"

Without hesitation, he said, "Catnip. I could use the extra boost."

I had to surmise, catnip to Milo was like caffeine to me. "Coming right up." In the back, I pulled out the floral china teapot and filled the infuser with a special blend from my mom. I needed to give her a call, but so much had been happening since movie night that I hadn't made the time. The kettle whistled and as I was pouring, I stopped midstream. Was she a witch too, or was Dad? Aunt Mimi had insinuated we were not the only witches in the family. I promised myself I was going to call her tonight, just to say hi and not to pump her for information. I finished pouring the tea and set the kettle aside. Once the tray with Milo's treat, my cup, and a small plate of cookies was ready to go out front, I put another cup on the tray, just in case I had company.

I stepped into the storefront and paused. Aunt Mimi was sitting in a chair near the window and Milo was perched on the table. They looked as if they were having a pleasant visit.

"Just in time for tea, Aunt Mimi." I made sure a sunny smile was on my face and my voice bright so as not to show I was upset by the way she had left earlier, even though it had shaken me.

"You summoned me again, but I understand you didn't follow the book but made up something off the top of your head."

This was great news. Maybe I didn't need to read the book after all. "I was just fooling around."

"My dear niece, it is best to have a firm foundation before you go rogue. What would the council say?"

That was confusing. Why would the town council even know that I was being creative? And that was so much better than rogue.

"Would they care?" I set the tray down and poured a cup of tea, passing it to Aunt Mimi. Before I could take my cup and sit, I tossed Milo's ball to the floor, and he pounced on it, rolling over and around with it clutched between his front paws.

"The council cares about everything a witch does, or doesn't do for that matter." She sipped her tea. "Excellent choice. One of your mother's blends?"

I nodded, pleased that she recognized it. Mom had a gift for blending different leaves. "Before we get back to why I wanted you to come over, is my mom a witch?"

"Not like you or me. It comes from the Michaels' side, but she is very intuitive and I think if she wanted to develop her skills, she could flourish as one. But your father is. Although he doesn't practice the craft, preferring to live life as a mortal." She shook her head. Disappointment about her brother was apparent.

"How old were you when you knew you were, you know, special?"

She smiled. "I think I always knew. There were *so* many things that mere coincidence couldn't explain, but when I was in my mid-twenties, the book found me, just as it did you. My mother guided me, but back then, it wasn't as widely accepted as it is now. In the witch community, people knew you were one, and magic was used extensively. I'm sure by now you've talked with Nikki about her abilities."

I nodded. There was nothing my aunt didn't know about me and my best friend. We had spent summers in Pembroke roaming the beach together. And when I got older, my parents moved inland to Pine Valley, about an hour away. How they could have left the beach was beyond me.

"You girls were always like two halves of a whole." She gave me an assessing look. "Still are." She finished the last of her tea and set the floral cup on the tray. "Why did you want to see me?"

Before I could think about what I wanted to say or how to say it, I blurted out, "I'm worried that Gage is going to arrest you for Flora's murder."

Her brow furrowed, and her smile fell away. "Why on earth would he do that? I've never harmed a living soul; it's part of being a good witch. If I had wanted to, it certainly wouldn't have been something as gruesome as hitting her over the head with a bat. To me, that suggests a man."

"Or a fit of rage. Since the bat was small, it had to have been forgotten after Little League practice." I looked around, remembering what Nikki had said earlier about people on the sidewalk listening. I dropped my voice. "He has the papers with the blackmail amounts and names and since you're on the top of the list, and you were with her almost at the moment she died, it's natural he's going to have to question you."

"This list you mention, who else is on it? The actual murderer has to be on there. Since I know it wasn't me."

"Aunt Mimi, just tell me why she wanted to extort money from you. What was such a secret that she thought you'd pay to keep it quiet?"

She dropped her head and studied the floor as if the rug had the most fascinating pattern. "I can't. It concerns Nate and me. Without him here, I'm not free to speak. We decided together and if there's a change, we have to decide that together too."

"I know that you and Nate have been dating forever, but I'm sure he'd never want your freedom to be put in jeopardy."

"He wouldn't, but until he comes in from his fishing trip today, I won't say a word."

An unfamiliar chill raced over my body. Not the kind where I was cold, but something more sinister. "Then we'll wait for him." I stood up, eager to get Aunt Mimi out the door and home before whatever had settled over me like a heavy wool blanket on a humid summer day made itself known.

As she stood up from the chair, the door opened and Gage walked in with Officer Peabody right behind him. Gage's face was grim and his gaze landed on Mimi.

"I'm glad I found you. Mimi Michaels, I'm sorry to say I'm taking you to the station to question you for the murder of Flora Gray."

And there it was. Gage was taking my aunt to the police station to be questioned for the murder of Flora. How could he do that to her?

Chapter 12
Gage

Lily stepped in between her aunt and me as she demanded, "Gage, have you lost your mind?"

I knew this wasn't going to go favorably with Lily, but I had to do my job. Although I didn't feel like I had to justify what I was doing, I did anyway. Mimi Michaels had been a part of my life since I met her niece when we were little squirts. I kept the handcuffs secured to the back of my belt. Keeping them out of sight might help Lily's temper. Not that I blamed her. This was an untenable situation.

"I'm sorry, Mimi. I have to follow the evidence and procedure."

She stepped around Lily and patted my cheek. "It's alright. I have nothing to worry about. I didn't kill Flora and once you hear my side of the story, I'm sure you'll believe me, too."

I quickly read her rights and asked if she wanted Lily to call her lawyer. It wasn't wise that she come in for questioning without someone there to protect her interests. If my boss wasn't pressuring me, I wouldn't have even come to the bookshop. But he wanted someone arrested, and he didn't care if it was the wrong person. At least the community wouldn't lose faith in our ability to solve the crime.

"Lily, call Nate and let him know what happened and then find me a lawyer and have them meet us at the police station." She looked Gage in the eye. "You will wait for a lawyer to show up before asking questions, right?"

I felt like a jerk. My heart was heavy as I nodded. "We'll give you time to talk with your lawyer before we begin formal questioning."

"Gage."

Lily's sharp tone stopped me in my tracks. I didn't want to meet her gaze. I had been on the receiving end before when she was furious, and this was bound to be worse.

Mimi said, "Lily. Stop. Gage has a job to do, and as I just told you, I've been withholding details that might help the case. You can't be mad because he's following procedure."

"I can and I am." Lily's face didn't soften, nor did the fire in her eyes.

But this was a look I hadn't seen before. I noticed she flexed her fingers in and out of a fist a few times as if she were preparing for a few rounds in a boxing ring. While she did, she was taking deep breaths. I had never seen her like this before. "Other than the obvious, are you okay? Do you need a drink of water?"

Her shoulders sagged. "No. I don't need anything to drink."

I wanted to wrap my arms around her. This was by far the worst thing I had ever done to her, and by the stars, I hoped it would be the last.

"Call Nikki. With her reporter contacts, she might know who the best lawyers in the county are. And then call one." I lightly clasped my arm on Mimi's forearm. "Ready?"

Her voice wavered. "You don't have to put handcuffs on me?"

"No. As long as you don't disappear into thin air." I hoped my light tone would crack the tension that hung heavy in the air.

"I haven't done that in years, and for the record, cuffs wouldn't do anything if I was to go poof." Her laugh helped to lighten my heart even if it hadn't changed the look on Lily's face.

"Gage."

My name was like a snarl from her lips. "There are several strong suspects besides Aunt Mimi. And I'll share what I know later tonight. With any luck, my aunt and I will forgive this slight error in judgment."

Mimi leaned closer. "She's just being protective. Don't worry. Her temper flares, and then logic will set in and you two will be back to being closer than straw on a broomstick."

Interesting analogy, but I'd take all the hope I could get right now. I took one last look at Lily. "See you at the station in a bit?"

"Absolutely."

As Mimi and I walked out of The Cozy Nook Bookshop with Peabody holding the door, Jill Dilly walked in. I gave her a polite nod as she stared, wide-eyed. This was sure to hit the gossip trail as soon as she left the shop. It wasn't hard to guess what she was thinking. She smirked in Mimi's direction, and a flash of annoyance flared through me. This could just as easily have been Jill if someone hadn't vouched for her location at the time of Flora's death.

Mimi held her head up high and sailed past Jill with a quick hello and a flutter of her fingertips, then got into the back seat of my car. I had opted to bring a dark sedan instead of the cruiser to keep some of Mimi's dignity intact. Only after I drove away did I see her in the rearview mirror sag against the seat back.

"What happens next?"

I could hear the tremor of trepidation in her

voice and wanted to reassure her. "Once we get to the station, we'll get settled in a conference room and wait for your lawyer to arrive."

"I won't have to talk right away?" She was staring out the window, watching the buildings slip by as we grew closer to our destination.

"No. I want you to have the chance to speak with your attorney, and then we'll talk about what happened that night and the few days leading up to it." She didn't respond. In the mirror I saw her nod. I couldn't feel any lower. It was as if I had my own mother in the back of the car. My thoughts returned to Lily. I knew why she was upset with me, and at some point we'd have to talk about the line between family and friends and duty to the badge.

I clenched the steering wheel tighter when I remembered the look on her face, like she could chew me up and spit me out and not think twice.

Peabody looked over at me. "What's eating you? Your girlfriend's ticked off and you don't know how to fix it?"

Lily, his girlfriend? Now where had Peabody gotten that idea? "It's not like that between me and Lily."

She continued to look at my profile, and I refused to turn her way. "Okay, if that's your story. But the looks you two give each other say otherwise."

"What?" I sputtered. How did Lily look at me? "I don't look at her any differently than I look at you."

With a shoulder shrug, she said, "If you say so."

I slowed the car and turned into the parking lot. It wouldn't surprise me if Lily was right behind us. That woman was a force unlike any other, and I swear if she put her mind to it, she could turn the tide away from the shore.

From the back seat, Mimi said, "Just curious. Whatever we talk about is confidential. You won't tell my family, will you?"

This surprised me. I parked the car in my spot and turned in my seat. "Mimi, you know that all secrets eventually come out. And what could be so terrible that you don't want Lily to know?"

"I never said it was terrible, just personal." She tried to open the door but discovered there was no handle on it. "I guess I need to wait for you."

I got out and came around the back side of the vehicle and opened the door, extending my hand to her.

With a tap on my arm, she snapped, "I'm not some old woman who needs help."

I wanted to sigh, but realized her inner fortitude was the same trait that I loved in her niece. I pointed to the walkway. "After you, ma'am."

I was in my office when I heard Lily's voice echo down the hall. The clerk at the desk buzzed me, and I was already moving to the door.

"Gage."

She rushed into the room and as much as I had hoped to see a smile on her pretty face, it was all business. "Lily. Did you find a lawyer for your aunt?"

"Of course I did. But that's not why I'm here. I have some new information for you to consider before you start to question an innocent woman."

"Won't be the first or last time I ask questions of someone who's innocent. It's how I get to the truth. But in this case, there is powerful evidence that points in your aunt's direction."

She popped her hands on her hips. "Like what?"

"Lil, I can't tell you that, at least not right now." I gestured for her to sit down. She hitched her bag a little higher on her shoulder and perched on the wooden chair across from my desk. I came around and tried to catch her eye, but she looked anyplace other than at me. This was so not good.

She leaned forward. "You can't tell me what you think you know about Aunt Mimi. But I know you know about the fifty-k with her name next to it on Flora's list. But I told you how we overheard Teddy Roberts say everyone in town was better off now that she was dead. Doesn't that make you wonder why? And where did the money come from? I'm going to guess that Jill, Marshall, and Teddy had been paying her money to keep her mouth shut on stuff, too. I'm sure my aunt told Flora to forget about her paying anything for blackmail."

I folded my hands and leaned forward. "What happened with Jill Dilly in your shop after we left?"

There was that smile I'd been looking for. The knowing grin continued to spread, and she smacked her hand on the desk. "I knew you'd be curious."

"You have a way of getting people to talk about themselves and not even realize how much information they've told you. I would bet my last dollar, you got something out of Jill that made the conversation worthwhile."

"At first, when she came in, she had questions about my aunt and what you had said about the case. I never came right out and told her I knew anything from you. And I certainly didn't tell her about the list."

"Good." My fingers itched to take notes, but this needed to be a straightforward conversation. I'd write it all down later. "Was she shopping or do you think she was being nosy, maybe saw the car and decided to wander in?"

"She was looking for travel books. Said she and a special friend were planning on taking an extensive trip. I'm going to guess that's Marshall. They've always seemed to be flirty at movie night when they've both come."

"Where and when was the trip going to happen?"

"Europe primarily, and as soon as they did some research, she was going to book the tickets. She felt as if they'd be coming into some money soon." She cocked a brow. "If they paid blackmail and came forward, would they get the money back?"

That was an interesting question and, once again, I marveled at how her mind worked. "It would be hard to prove that the money we found was indeed money Jill might have paid Flora. Even with her name on that list and a dollar amount, it could have been a fine for an overdue book and a misplaced decimal point."

That made Lily actually laugh out loud. "You don't believe that?"

"Of course not, but again, blackmail in itself is a crime. It would be up to the district attorney and she'd need to produce proof of the money paid. With Flora dead, that could be tricky unless she had a video or something else really solid."

"That would go for anyone, like Marshall and Teddy, too? And couldn't they corroborate her story?"

Her brain was on fire with questions, and it impressed me. "It could be considered a conflict of interest and that might not hold up. I can't say for sure what will happen to the money." I watched as she pursed her lips, thinking.

"Did she say anything else while she was in the shop?"

"Only that she and Marshall plan on coming

to movie night on Monday." Her eyes lit up. "I mentioned it to you earlier. I'm gathering my suspects at the library again on Monday night and by then I'll know who killed Flora. You need to plan on being there so you can arrest the actual killer."

My mouth went dry. The idea that Lily was really going to set up a murder party to flush out the killer was insane. Even if I was going through the motions of questioning Mimi, I didn't believe she had done anything wrong. Murder was either premeditated or a crime of passion. If she had been planning on offing Flora, she would never have committed the crime in close proximity to Lily, and if it had been a crime of passion, why use a baseball bat? That's when it hit me.

"Lily, when you got to the library to set up, do you remember seeing any kids who might have come from ball practice?"

She tapped her lips and tipped her head to the side. Then her finger traced the outline of something in midair. What was she doing?

"No. I got there around five thirty, so more than likely kids would be home, getting ready to have dinner. But someone could have been there earlier in the day. That would be simple enough. Just call the Little League coach and see if there was a practice or game. If not, it's going to be harder to figure out who the bat belongs to."

She didn't need to point out that obvious fact.

With a snap of her fingers, Lily said, "What if the bat wasn't left by accident and instead had been planted there for the specific purpose of a premeditated attack?"

"That's exactly what I just thought, too." I held up my hand and smacked her with a high five. Before I could continue, Peabody popped around the doorjamb.

"Detective, Ms. Michaels' lawyer is here."

Lily's smile faded. "Tell my aunt I'll be waiting when you're done interrogating her."

Chapter 13
Lily

I sat on the hard wooden bench, well-worn from all the years people had sat here, waiting. I glanced at the wall clock. Two hours had felt like an eternity with Aunt Mimi and her lawyer undergoing questioning with Gage and Peabody. I wished I could be an observer, like in the movies, in a small room, watching and listening via a one-way mirror. Since that wasn't an option, I just needed to be patient and wait.

The door banged open and Nate burst through it. His hair was matted from where his baseball cap usually sat, which was now in his hands. I lifted my hand in greeting and patted the space next to me.

He hurried over and sat down, his eyes scanning the room. I knew he was hoping to see his mermaid.

"Where is she? Why did they bring her in for questioning? There is no way she could have hurt Flora, even if she was a bloodsucking leech."

I placed my hand on his arm. "Nate. Take a breath and try to calm down. I'll tell you what I know and we can go from there." I pointed to the hallway. "She's in a conference room down the hall and I got a lawyer to come in."

He twisted his hat in his calloused hands. It was easy to see how much he cared for my aunt. It was as plain as the nose on my face. He loved her with every fiber of his soul. "Is he any good?"

I had to hold back a smile as he immediately went to the lawyer being a man. He was old-fashioned in some ways, and this was one of them. "Nikki recommended Jordan King. She's a former prosecutor at the district attorney's office in Portland. Extremely well respected and was happy to do Nikki a favor since they've known each other a long time."

He gave a bob of his head. "Good credentials." His eyes never left the hallway as he said, "Mimi's lawyer is a woman?"

"Yes. She has the reputation of the shark that great whites are afraid of." I thought he'd appreciate the ocean reference.

He grinned for a fraction of a second before his face turned grim again.

We sat quietly. I knew he needed to have something else to think about other than what might be happening down the hall.

"I know you need to hear how this came about. Aunt Mimi had come down to the shop. I had something I wanted to discuss with her." I wasn't sure if I should talk to Nate about my summoning spell or that I really used it so I could pump her for information about why Mimi wouldn't tell me what had happened with Flora, so I skipped all of that. "Gage came in and told her he needed to bring her into the station for questioning and there was a chance they could place her under arrest for Flora's murder."

Nate turned and looked at me. The muscle in his jaw popped. I had only seen that look once before and it, too, had involved my aunt. It was several years ago, and I didn't remember the specifics, but it was his fiercely protective mode.

"She didn't do it." His statement was more like a growl. He got up and crossed the room to where the receptionist sat. "I need to talk to Detective Erikson. I'm here to confess to the murder of Flora Gray."

I jumped up from the bench and raced across the room. "Nate, what are you doing? Confessing to something like murder will only cloud the issue. And they'll stop looking for the real killer."

He shook his head. "I will not let my mermaid be charged with the crime." He pointed to the phone. "Buzz the detective."

This was the craziest and most romantic thing I had ever seen. But it was also so wrong.

Gage wouldn't buy into this nonsense. He was smarter than that.

A door at the end of the hallway opened, and Gage strode into the lobby. He gave me a curt nod and focused his attention on Nate.

"I heard you needed to speak with me?"

My breath caught. Could he really take Nate seriously?

"I killed Flora. Mimi had nothing to do with it." He took a step forward and held out his wrists. "Arrest me and let Lily take her home."

"I'm not about to arrest you. There is no way you killed Flora, since there are several people who said you were in the conference room when Mimi went outside." He took Nate's arm and steered the old fisherman, who seemed to have aged twenty years since he walked in, to a chair. "You need to trust me."

"But Mimi did nothing wrong. Flora was the witch who was putting the squeeze on many people in this town. We're allowed to live our lives in private."

Gage knelt down next to Nate. "I agree with

you. If you give me about ten minutes, we're just wrapping up and you can take Mimi home."

"You're not going to throw her in the pokey?"

I hid a smile with the back of my hand at his corny word for jail. But I waited to see what he'd say next.

"No. She's not under arrest and is free to go, but I might need to bring her back in for more questions, so it would be best to stay in town."

Nate tapped his fingers on his brow in a half salute. "You got it, boss."

Gage gave me a tentative smile, as if testing the waters. I wasn't mad at him anymore, but I wished he had handled the whole thing better. Especially when Jill Dilly came into the shop.

"I need to talk to you before I go home."

He quirked a brow. "About?"

"A conversation I had earlier today." My eyes darted to Nate, trying to convey I didn't want to say any more in front of him. There were a couple more tidbits I wanted to share with him about Jill.

"Want to get a pizza and go to the park? I need to get out of here for a while."

At the park, we shouldn't have anyone around to overhear our conversation, and Gage could talk more freely about the case and we could compare notes. "Sounds good. But I'm picking the toppings tonight."

His smile went from tentative to a full, toothy grin. "Deal."

True to his word, Gage escorted Aunt Mimi to the lobby with her lawyer, Ms. King, right behind them. She hadn't been what I expected when we talked on the phone. She was dressed in a tailored navy-blue suit, coordinating perfectly with a blouse of navy and white polka dots, but it was her high heels that didn't fit with the typical attorney image.

Nate jumped up and pulled Mimi into a hug. Seeing them together reminded me their love was ageless and forever. It had taken him years to convince her to go out with him when they were in their forties, but once that happened, they had been together ever since. I often wondered why they never tied the knot, but if they were happy, who was I to ask questions?

Ms. King shook Gage's hand. "Detective Erikson, if you need to ask my client additional questions, I want to be present."

"Absolutely. Thank you for coming in so quickly today. I'm sure you have a busy schedule."

A twinge of jealousy piqued as it seemed she held Gage's hand a little longer than necessary. I quickly reminded myself he was single and could shake or hold anyone's hand he wanted. Turning away, I picked up my shoulder bag from the bench and smiled as Nate took Aunt Mimi's hand and kissed her cheek.

She took a step away from Nate and looked at me. She opened her arms to wrap them around me, just like she did when I was young. I held on tight and kissed her cheek. "I'm going to find out who did this. Don't worry."

Looking into my eyes, I could see the fear

that lingered in hers. "No. Let Gage do his job. I couldn't bear it if anything happened to you."

"Aunt Mimi, I'll be smart. Besides," I whispered in her ear. "I'm a witch, remember?"

With a shake of her head, she laughed. "You can't even light a candle."

With my sauciest of winks, I chuckled. "Oh yes, I can. I finally mastered that task, and the location and summoning spells. I'm on fire."

"You have much more to learn before you can protect yourself from humans that go bump in the night." She clasped my hands and held tight. The chill of hers shocked me. Her touch had always been warm and comforting. I glanced at Gage and wondered what they had said between them to affect her this way. "Promise me you'll be careful."

She knew there was no talking me out of checking on things. So the most she could say was to keep a watchful eye. "Promise. Nikki will go with me whenever I need her and"—I tossed a glance at Gage, still talking with the lovely Jordan King—"he will look out for me, too."

"I'm not worried when you're with someone, but when you venture off on your own, that mischief can find you."

Nate said, "Are you ready to go home?"

She placed her hand on his cheek. "One more minute."

"Take all the time you need, mermaid." His voice was soft and tender, and I knew he'd wait for her as long as needed.

"You must come by the house in the morning and wear the necklace I gave you. I'm going to add some enhancements to it. I'm certain you're going to be off asking questions. If you're not able to protect yourself, I'm going to do all I can to help you."

My aunt was the sweetest lady in Pembroke, and except for my mom, maybe anywhere. "I'll be by around eight, if that works?" I glanced at Nate. "Are you going lobstering tomorrow?"

Mimi looked at Nate. "Of course he is. There's no reason for him to stay in town. Besides, I was hoping he'd get a big one for you and the handsome detective to share tomorrow night."

I hugged her again, and this time my voice wasn't soft and sweet, but firm. "Stop pushing, Aunt Mimi."

She snickered and called out, "Gage, we're going to take off now." He came over. Was it my imagination or was it hard for him to tear away from Ms. King? Oh, it was a good thing my eyes were brown because if they were hazel now, they'd be bright green with jealousy.

"I'm sorry about everything today, Mimi, but I'm glad we cleared up a few things. But be careful who you talk to, or better yet, don't tell anyone what happened here." He placed his hand on my shoulder. "Not even this lovely lady."

I perked up. Did he just say I was lovely? That was a win.

"Don't worry, Gage. My lips are sealed." For added effect, she pretended to be zipping her lips. "Not a word out of me until you say I can talk."

"Good." He looked at Nate. "Be careful driving home."

I thought that was an odd thing to say to him, but whatever. This whole day had been annoying on many levels.

Gage touched my arm. "Give me five minutes and then call in a pizza. I'll be ready to leave in fifteen."

Aunt Mimi watched our exchange, and the moment Gage walked away, she grinned. "Now that's better. You should definitely ask him for lobster tomorrow night. Nate will make sure you have the best of the day's catch."

I kissed her cheek at the subtle reference to how she thought Gage was the best catch in town. She loved talking in her version of code. "You're incorrigible."

After fifteen minutes, Gage walked into the deserted lobby and grinned at me as he noticed my legs up on the bench. "Are you ready to pick up the pizza and head to the park?"

"More than ready. I'm starved. Lunch was a million years ago." I looped my arm through his and chuckled. "You do know I'm going to pump you for details about everything."

He wiggled his eyebrows and laughed. "And you know I will not tell you anything that's confidential." He pushed open the door, and I stepped through, certain I could get what I needed to keep sleuthing.

The air in the park was cool, and I was glad I had a sweater. But the sun was still out, and it offered a modicum of warmth. I was pleased to see we were the only people headed to the picnic tables. Gage had the pizza box in one hand, and I was carrying two fountain drinks and a mound of paper towels. The pizza was good, but I could easily end up wearing something like cheese or toppings on my blouse and with that grease, I'd have a hard time getting it clean.

I wondered if Nikki had a spell for hard to remove stains. Being a kitchen witch, she might have some interesting options. I made a mental note to ask her tomorrow.

Gage gestured to a table closer to where the

best ocean view was, and he knew it was one of my favorite places to watch the waves.

"You know me too well." I smiled and followed him to the table.

After we got settled and each had a slice of pizza in front of us, I sipped my drink, wondering how best to approach the investigation. Not finding a soft opening, I stopped tiptoeing around the topic.

"What made you need to drag Aunt Mimi down to the police station and question her like a common criminal who had killed Flora? Besides the fact that she was found standing over the body and her name was on the blackmail ledger?"

"Going for the jugular tonight?" But the amused smile on his lips and in his eyes said he'd expected me to be direct.

"We have a lot to talk about and I just want to know why." In my mind, there was no sense in making small talk when he'd known this was the only thing I really wanted to discuss.

"I can't give you the details, but it didn't look

good with those two things and we found her fingerprints on the bat."

"Of course you did. She said it was propped near Flora's head and started to fall, so Mimi grabbed it before it could hit her."

He nodded, as if confirming that part of her story. "But that was vital information that was withheld during our initial conversation. If it wasn't for my relationship with your family, Aunt Mimi would be sitting in a jail cell right now."

Chapter 14
Lily

I started choking on a piece of pepperoni when Gage said the evidence had been strong enough to lock her up for the night. Sputtering, I said, "But lots of people in town hated Flora. My aunt was hardly the first to refuse to cave into her demands. Or was she?"

Gage seemed to weigh his answer carefully, and I knew he was going to tell me something important.

"As far as we can tell, based on checking the facts, your aunt was the only person who refused. That means we have a lot of suspects who were paying her and monthly, too."

"She was opening a vein every month and demanding payment?" My shoulders slumped as I processed the information. It was a steady flow of cash for her and a steady drain for what, ten or fifteen people? "How long do you think this was going on?"

Gage wiped his mouth with a napkin, but missed a spot of sauce on his cheek. I reached out and wiped it off and he smiled in thanks.

"It's hard to say. Based on the amount of cash we found in her home, I'd guess for quite a while."

I thought of the money stacks I had discovered under her bed and it was a good amount, but what if there had been more? "How much exactly?"

He studied the fresh slice in his hands and I knew he was stalling, trying to decide just what he could or should say. His voice was very low, almost inaudible. "North of a quarter of a mill."

"There wasn't that much cash under the bed."

Looking around the empty park, he said, "There were other hiding places."

When I opened my mouth to ask a question, he shook his head.

"I can't tell you any more than that. You just need to trust me. She was bilking a lot of people out of a ton of money."

I chewed my lower lip and wondered how she had gotten her nose into people's lives so deeply that she could extract money from them, all to protect secrets. And what kind of secrets could the people in Pembroke need to hide? This was insane. "I guess you never really know your neighbors."

His eyebrow quirked as his eyes locked on mine. "Meaning?"

"It's just, how could so many people have secrets that they'd pay to keep them from coming to light?"

He tipped his head and gave me an intense

look without blinking. "Don't you have things you wouldn't want everyone to know?"

For a moment I thought about what I might want no one else to know and the only real secret I had was my feelings for him—well, and that I was witch and talked to a cat, who talked back. But would I pay to keep that quiet? No. Could it be slightly embarrassing if he found out? He might think I was silly when he didn't return the sentiment. But no, it wasn't something I'd pay to keep in the shadows.

"Sure. we all have some things we'd rather not let everyone know. My gran used to say, 'we don't need to air our dirty laundry.' But it's nothing so horrible or embarrassing that I'd have to pay to keep it quiet." I leaned forward. "Do you have secrets?"

Gage lifted a shoulder and refocused on a slice of pizza. "Nah, I'm an open book."

The way he avoided my gaze told a different story. He, like everyone, had something that he'd rather keep on the down-low. I guessed it was part of human nature, but I never thought about it until now.

"Are you going to tell me what happened with Aunt Mimi?"

He avoided my eyes. "Nope."

"Come on." I poked his shoulder. He laughed and still didn't look at me. I knew that stance. There was a lot going on with the investigation and no way he was going to give me the lowdown. "So, we're done talking about the case?"

"Yup." He slurped his soda. "Rumor has it you're getting a special delivery of lobster tomorrow and I'm invited."

"How did you...?" The question drifted on the breeze. Aunt Mimi was doing her best to play matchmaker. She'd had a soft spot for Gage forever and always insisted we were like two peas in a pod.

"Aunt Mimi?"

"Of course. What time should I come over? I'll pick up dessert."

"Six. I'll need to swing by the boat and pick up the lobster after I close the shop."

"It's a date." Gage's face flushed a deep shade of pink the moment the words were out of his mouth. "You know, not like a date-date, but a couple of best friends hanging out, slurping up butter with hunks of crustaceans."

I knew exactly what he meant, but I wished it were a proper date. "No worries and if anything comes up, just call." I picked up the last slice of pizza, eager to get home and call Nikki and talk to Milo—and not necessarily in that order.

The moment I walked through the back door, Milo trotted into the kitchen. "I was getting hungry." He swished his tail, which I was sure meant he was annoyed with me.

"I think I liked it better when you couldn't talk." I pulled the container of kitty kibble from the cabinet and poured some in his bowl.

"That's how much you know. I've always

been talking. You just couldn't understand until you opened the darn book."

It sounded like he muttered, 'stubborn woman,' under his kitty breath. But I didn't want to press the point since I had questions and maybe he could help me find the answers. Antagonizing him wasn't the best course of action. To help take the sharp edge from his mood of waiting on his dinner, I opened a can of tuna, sprinkled the dry kibble with the juice, and then mixed in a couple of hunks into his dinner.

He looked at the bowl after I placed it on the ground and then at me. "Peace offering accepted."

While he munched, I went to my office to get the chalkboard and chalk and returned to the kitchen. I wanted to jot down all I knew about events leading up to Flora's death and everything that had happened since. But this time I'd take a picture on my cell and wipe the board clean. Just in case.

I sat in the chair with the board in front of

me. Milo had hopped onto the table and eyed the board and then me.

"You're going to do this again?"

His grumble-laced words sent goose bumps over my arms. I remembered that someone was in our home and after ransacking it, wiped my notes from this very board.

Taking a deep breath, I said, "Yes. You must have known they took Aunt Mimi to the police station for questioning. It took hours and although Gage released her, I need to clear her name. The cloud of suspicion hanging over her is something I can't ignore."

Milo licked his paw. The next step was to wash his face. "I saw Gage put her in his car. He didn't arrest her."

"No. But if things don't change, that could be next." I could hear the fear creep into my voice. I sat up a little straighter and wrote all that I knew and remembered.

Flora – blackmail ten to fifteen residents

Money over a quarter million dollars in her home

Aunt Mimi—secret fifteen-k
Baseball bat at scene
No kids at library
Hard candy wrapper at scene
Movie night: Jill, Marshall, Teddy, Meredith, Nikki, Steve, Nate, Mimi, and me
The gentlemen from Colin Senior Living Community—not likely suspects

I circled the number twelve suspects and then crossed it out and subtracted the seniors, leaving ten. I couldn't remember all the names on Flora's list, but I put a checkmark next to Jill, Teddy, Marshall, and Aunt Mimi. Those I remembered. I leaned back. "What about the baseball bat? Whose was it and why was it left there?"

"That's something you might never find out," Milo was quick to remind me, and I hated that he was probably right.

"I need to dig deeper into Jill, Teddy, and Marshall. They are the most likely suspects, and what about the fourth person at Teddy's place the other night? Who was he?" I didn't add him to the suspect list since he wasn't at the library. But then, just because I hadn't seen him there doesn't mean he wasn't. I added him.

Under the movie night list, I wrote: *Mystery man?*

I tapped the chalk on my chin. What was missing?

"Are you going to add Jill's mysterious trip? And whoever she might go with? That seems odd, given that she mentioned she's never traveled outside the state of Maine."

"Good point, Milo." I rubbed the top of his head. "Nikki and I need to take a drive out to Marshall's place, but I can't think of a good reason to be out there after dinner."

"Doesn't he have a farm stand? Say you're looking for something that he has there. Blueberries or something."

"Rhubarb. The market never carries it and I can say I need some for a pie for my dinner guest tomorrow night and maybe he'll have strawberries too."

"Whoa, girl. No need to go getting all elaborate with your story. Stick to the fact that you need rhubarb and the bit about the market. Besides, he might know you're not the best baker."

That's when I gave him a *cat who licked the cream bowl* smile. "But my best friend can make a pie rivaled by no one in town." I picked up my cell and called Nikki.

Before she could even say hello, I asked, "How do you feel about going out to Marshall's farm stand with me tonight in search of rhubarb and maybe strawberries? I could use a pie for dinner with Gage tomorrow night."

"Sure. Want me to pick you up so you can keep your eyes peeled for goings-on in town?"

I laughed. "I missed the entire blackmail scheme, so unless people are dancing in the streets and we can't avoid them, I might not notice."

"Not true. I'll see you in ten."

She disconnected, and I swiveled in the chair. "Is there a way to not erase this, but to anyone else it would look blank?"

Milo stood up and did his whole body

stretch. "Read the book and find out." He jumped down and slunk from the kitchen.

I called after him. "Is that your response to everything?"

He paused and looked over his shoulder. "Maybe." And then he turned and disappeared.

I thought about erasing the board, which was my original intent. Instead, I slipped it into the pantry cabinet and made sure the doors and windows were locked and pocketed my house keys. The last time someone had trashed my house and locked Milo in a closet, the house had been wide open. It was more my fault than the perp. My nonchalance was like rolling out the welcome mat.

In nine minutes, the sound of a horn toot in my driveway drew me to the door. I grabbed my shoulder bag and called out, "I'll be back soon." Milo didn't answer, so I secured the door and lightly ran down the back steps to Nikki's car.

She was grinning. The moment I got in and

buckled up, she asked, "So what are we really doing?"

"Drive and I'll fill you in. Today has been eye-opening." I took a moment to gather my thoughts and filled her in on Jill's visit to the bookshop, my aunt's questioning at the police station, dinner with Gage, and everything I had written on my murder board.

"Since we now know that Aunt Mimi's prints were the only ones found on the bat and as far as we know she's the only one who refused to pay the blackmail, it makes sense that one of the other blackmail victims is the real murderer."

She nodded. "And tell me why we're going to the farm stand?"

"Marshall is the next person we need to talk to. I want to find out what his motive might have been and if he's planning a trip. Maybe he's the person going with Jill."

"Then why isn't Gage out here talking to Marshall and not us?" She glanced at me. Her right eyebrow arched to an unnatural height.

"He has to follow the evidence and can't go

on a hunch." I stared out the window as we drove inland and entered farm country.

"Does he know we're going out here to question Marshall?"

"We're going to buy rhubarb, which I can't get at the market, so I can serve a strawberry rhubarb pie for dinner tomorrow night." I gave her my best innocent smile. "Can't fault a girl for trying to serve a nice dinner."

"Gage?"

I bobbed my head. "Yes, Nate is providing the lobster." I snapped my fingers. "I need to have Gage pick up the bread or something. He had offered to bring dessert, so this whole ploy will fall apart with my pie diversion. Maybe I should text him."

Nikki put a hand on my arm, and it stopped me from pulling out my phone. "Wait to see what happens with Marshall. If you need to stretch the truth after, then okay, but for now, just let things ride."

I hadn't figured out what I wanted to say, exactly. Hopefully winging it would work out.

About five minutes later I noticed the sign for Marshall's farm stand up ahead. I took a deep breath and exhaled.

Nikki glanced my way. "Don't worry. I've got your back and with a little magic to help."

"I'm not sure your magic can help us, but sure." To be honest, I knew my magic would not be useful either. Finding something, lighting a candle, and summoning a person wasn't exactly an arsenal of magic at our disposal. It was too bad I hadn't opened the book sooner. Can't worry about what I should have done.

Once the car was parked, I noticed there were two other people looking over the produce placed artfully on the beds of old-fashioned hay wagons. The low, flat surfaces were filled with baskets overflowing with lettuce, cucumbers, green beans, strawberries, and blueberries along with a basket of rhubarb. At least that part of the plan was working out perfectly. The next wagon had cut flowers in old milk buckets and hats that looked like buckets that once held that paste they use when hanging sheetrock. I wanted to check those out, too. Nothing like a fresh flower to transform a space. I might even pick some up for the shop.

I glanced at Nikki, my hand on the door handle. "Ready?"

"Wait. Maybe we should have a code word." Her eyes were wide, which quickly dispelled the idea she was joking.

"We're in a public place. Nothing is going to happen." I hoped my voice reassured her, since now that she had brought it up, maybe we should develop some sort of system between us. This would not be our last foray into poking around. "Come on. We'll get attention just by sitting here." I nodded in the direction of Marshall, who had just caught sight of the car, and by the scowl on his face, he was not happy to see us.

Chapter 15
Lily

We strolled across the gravel parking lot and one person who had been shopping was now carrying an overflowing paper bag to her car. That left one additional shopper.

Marshall looked at us as we approached. His eyes widened for a fraction of a second before returning to normal. If I hadn't been watching him watch us, I would have missed it. It was something I'd have to tell Nikki on the way back to town.

I lifted my hand in greeting and smiled. "Hi,

Marshall. I'm glad you're still open."

His gaze darted to Nikki and back to me as he licked his lips nervously. "Until the sun goes down. It's a farmer's life."

"At least in winter you get more sleep." I cringed at my quip, but he ignored it.

"What can I help you ladies with tonight?" He glanced at the sun slipping toward the horizon. "Be closing up soon."

I looked over my shoulder at the western sky. I had plenty of time to browse and casually ask a few questions too.

"Everything looks amazing. Do you grow everything here on your farm or do you work with others and sell their produce and flowers?" I was pretty pleased with myself, getting him to focus on the wagons.

He walked around to the opposite side, where Nikki and I were admiring the lettuce.

"Mostly from my fields, but the flowers are from Wee Flower Farm. Dee Skorput has the best luck. When I try, I get weeds."

I smiled at what I thought was a joke. But

when I saw his face was expressionless, my smile faded. "Everyone has a talent for something and by the looks of these veggies, I'd say that's where yours lie." I picked up a head of lettuce and he handed me a shopping basket that seemed to appear out of thin air. "Thank you."

I added a large deep-red tomato, thinking how one slice would hang over from the sides of a sandwich and it made my mouth water. But I quickly reminded myself I wasn't really here to buy produce.

"Marshall, are you going to come to the library on Monday night? We're going to run the movie we missed."

"I'm not sure. The last time didn't turn out that great." He gave me a serious look. "What are you thinking? Maybe we should hold off on starting that up until after the person who killed poor Flora is arrested."

What had he just said? It almost sounded like sorrow in his voice. Poor Flora. The words ran around and around as I tried to dissect if it was real or manufactured sadness. Now I was going to try a different approach. I added a bunch of radishes to my basket. "I didn't realize you and Flora were close."

"We weren't. But nobody deserves to die like that." He shook his head as he looked at the ground. It was easy to see he was genuinely sorry about her death. But even a murderer can have remorse.

"Who do you think killed her?" Nothing like jumping right into the thick of my questions.

His head came up sharply, and he said, "I have no idea. It's for the police to investigate, not for me to speculate. Is that why you came out here tonight? To try to see if I had anything to do with her being murdered?"

"No. Really. I'm having someone over for dinner tomorrow and I wanted to serve the best that I can. Nate is going to give me a couple of lobsters and fresh seafood deserves the best sides." I pointed to Nikki. "She's going to bake a pie for me."

He seemed to relax after I brought Nate into the picture. "Dinner with your fella?"

Nikki snorted and quickly looked away.

"I don't have a man in my life." I was quick to change the subject.

"Back when I was a young man, I remember what it was like to look at a pretty girl whom I wanted to spend time with. Trust me, he has that same look. I'm not so old that I don't remember."

My thoughts turned to Jill and my suspicion that she and Marshall were taking off on a romantic vacation together. "You're not old."

As I looked closely, it seemed as if I was really seeing him for the first time. He looked old. Like he had a tough life and it had caught up to him.

"I was a few years behind your aunt and Nate. I should think about retiring, but I don't know what I'd do with myself. I'll keep farming until they plant me in the ground."

"What about traveling? There must be places you'd like to see. Maybe travel with a friend, perhaps." I wasn't sure how smooth I was at trying to find out about this trip.

"No. That doesn't suit me. Other than driving to Portland or Bar Harbor, that's as far as I'm going to roam. I'm a Mainer and my hometown has all I need or want."

Unless he was lying, which I doubted, he wasn't planning to take a trip with Jill. I had one more chance to learn a little more.

"I saw Jill Dilly today. She came into my bookshop. She was picking up some travel books and said she was going with a friend. I just assumed it was you." The hook was baited now; I just needed to wait and see if he took it.

His face fell. "No. We're not that kind of friends."

Based on his reaction, he would have liked to be, though. "Marshall. It's none of my business, but have you ever asked her to have dinner with you? I know you drive her to the library for movie night. At least you have a couple of times. Maybe she's waiting for you to ask her on an actual date."

"Nah. She's got her cap set for someone, and it's not me." He pointed to Nikki and my baskets.

"Are you ready for me to ring you up? It's almost closing time."

I handed him my basket, and Nikki did the same. "Please reconsider coming on Monday. I think getting together is a good way to put this unpleasant incident behind us."

He gave me the total and bagged the items we had bought. I handed him the cash.

"I'll give it some thought, Lily. Thanks for your business."

I took the bag as he came around the side of the wagon. I swept my hand the length of the two wagons. "Do you need any help to put all this away?"

He gave me a rare smile. "No. I'll just hook the wagons to the tractor and head into the barn. But I appreciate the offer. You're a nice lady."

After saying our goodbyes, Nikki and I got back in the car for the return trip to my house. We rode is silence for several minutes. As we approached town, I was thinking of the murder board.

"You should come in and I'll add my notes to

the board and maybe you can see what I'm over-looking."

"I can't stay long. I have a pie to make—ac-tually two. I have enough fruit, so I'll whip up one for you and one for Steve. He loves my pie."

"That's not all he loves. I think one of these days he's going to pop a very important question."

Her laughter was infectious. "Fingers crossed it won't be long."

"What about you asking him?" Not that it was something I'd want to do, but it was an op-tion. We lived in the twenty-first century.

"Call me old-fashioned, but it's a moment I've dreamed of for a long time. I will not rush or spoil it by being pushy."

When Nikki pulled into the driveway, Gage was sitting on my back step. He looked at me as we unloaded my bag from the car.

"This is a surprise. What's going on?" He took the bag from my hands, and I unlocked the door. I looked over my shoulder and saw his face was taut. When we got inside, he took my hands and guided me to a chair.

"I wanted to tell you that someone broke into your aunt Mimi's house. She's okay, but it was almost a replay of what happened here. Except instead of locking Milo in a closet, someone whacked her on the head and put her in a closet and then ransacked her house."

My hand flew to my mouth and my heart sank. "Gage, is she?"

"She's fine. I would tell you if she wasn't. However, this gives some merit to whoever killed Flora must think Mimi has some evidence that could point to them."

"On the other hand, it also shows that it couldn't be my aunt. Does this mean she's off the suspect list?"

He nodded in agreement. "It pushes her way down."

Instantly, I relaxed. "I'm going to call her to check in. If you want to stay for something to drink, hang around."

He gave me a smile. "I'll be back tomorrow.

You and Nikki, I'm sure, have things to talk about."

If he knew what we were really up to, he wouldn't be so quick to leave. "You don't need to bring dessert tomorrow. We picked up some fruit and Nikki's making a pie for us."

His grin started in one corner of his mouth and slid to the other. "My taste buds are already preparing for it." He pretended to give a brief salute by tapping his fingers to his forehead. "I'll leave you ladies to enjoy the rest of your evening."

He closed the door, and I sank into the chair. "If you'll put the teakettle on, I'll call my aunt."

Nikki placed a comforting hand on my shoulder. "I'll fix you one of my blends. It will help you relax and focus on what we really need to work out—what happened with your aunt and, ultimately, who killed Flora."

I couldn't have agreed more. "Don't forget to add a splash of honey to my cup."

She pointed to my phone. "Call Mimi."

My aunt reassured me several times she was

fine, but she didn't see who bopped her over the head before getting shut in the closet. But somehow the person seemed gentle when they pushed her in there. It was just a feeling, but Aunt Mimi said the person might even have been sorry to have done it. This was something I was going to add to my board. Since I was zeroing in on Jill, her taking this impromptu vacation was definitely something to consider when looking at the clues.

I held the mug in my hands, warming them. I hadn't realized until that point that I was chilled. I sipped and sighed. Honey and the blend of tea were delicious. Nikki really had the golden touch for tea leaves. It dawned on me, that was part of her craft.

"I'm going to guess something just clicked in your ever-spinning brain." Nikki's tone was light and teasing.

"I just realized why your tea is always so good. It's the kitchen witch thing, isn't it?"

"Yes."

I appreciated she didn't pretend that it was no big deal. "Do you like being a witch?"

She seemed to think about my question or maybe on how best to answer it. "It's not like we have a choice. We are who we are. I had to embrace it and you need to also. Learn how to control it, use it, work it to your best advantage."

I audibly groaned. "The book is so dull and the spells are so hard."

"Stop thinking like an unmagical person."

At that moment, Milo entered the kitchen. "Nikki, I keep telling her to read the book."

Her mouth fell open. "You haven't finished it yet?"

Now I had two of them harping on me as well as Aunt Mimi. My defenses flared. "I'll get to it. Right now, I'm trying to keep my aunt out of prison." I closed my eyes and sipped my tea, but behind my lids I could picture the two of them looking at each other, shocked that I still hadn't finished the darn book. What was so special about it I needed to rush through the pages instead of mastering each spell at a single moment in time?

I regurgitated my thoughts almost verbatim. "Answer me this. Why is it so important I read the book before I master the spells one at a time?"

Milo and Nikki looked at each other. I realized they weren't going to answer me. I gave up. "We need to get back to the task at hand." I got up and pulled out the board from the closet and faced it toward Nikki and Milo. I began to talk and write at the same time.

"Marshall goes to the bottom of the suspect list. He came across as genuinely sad that Flora was killed. Even if he was paying her off, he didn't harm her." Next, I wrote Jill's name with an arrow to Marshall. "He likes Jill, but it seems Jill is interested in someone else since she's planning this trip with a friend." I added the air quotes for extra emphasis. "My guess, it's Teddy. Remember, he was riding with them the night of the murder. Which is odd since he lives in town." From Jill's name, I added an arrow pointing to Teddy's.

Nikki pointed to their three names. "This is a potential love triangle."

I held up my finger. "It is. But how might it connect to the blackmail scheme Flora was running?" I snapped my fingers. "Unless we go back to my original theory and they're in it together."

Chapter 16
Lily

The next morning, I swung by the library to chat with Meredith before opening the shop. Milo had taken off the minute I unlocked the back door. I was sure I'd see him later. He had a way of just showing up.

I pulled open the heavy old-fashioned wood doors to the town library. I had side-stepped the spot where Flora died but noticed someone had cleaned the blood from the cement. Entering the space was like the grand scale of my bookshop on steroids. The smell of new and old books mingled in the temperature-controlled air. The mood was lighter as I strolled through. Could it be Flora's death had changed the vibe of this space? I knew anything was possible.

I spied Meredith at the main desk. It was the place where Flora used to stand and keep an eagle eye on everyone in the library. But instead of watching the people browsing for their book or reading the newspaper, Meredith was busy looking at the computer. I gave her a wave in hopes she'd see me. I didn't want to startle her.

Success. She looked up and gave me a controlled smile, like the one she had perfected while working for Flora. "Lily, it's wonderful to see you had time to stop by. I expected you last night."

"I ran into a minor glitch. They took Aunt Mimi in for questioning regarding your boss' death."

Her mouth slacked, and her eyes grew wide. "Why? No one could think your aunt had anything to do with Flora's death. Mimi is one of the nicest people in town. At least she's always been nice to me."

I appreciated Meredith's support. "That's so kind of you. But her prints were on the bat and she was standing over the body. Gage said he had to follow the evidence."

"Was she arrested?"

"No. Just questioned, so all is fine now." I wasn't about to tell her what happened later with Aunt Mimi getting hit on the head and pushed into a closet.

She placed a hand over her heart and gave me a small smile. "Thank goodness." She held up a bowl of candy. "Butterscotch?"

I declined and said, "Are you sure it's okay to have movie night here on Monday? No concerns or issues? We'll make sure there are zero popcorn kernels on the floor and we'll put the garbage in the bin out back."

She placed a hand on my arm. "Please. I have no concerns when you're here. In fact. I've penciled in movie night once a month for the rest of the year. The second Monday of each month."

It pleased me she thought to do that. It was something I had asked Flora to do for the last several years. "Thank you."

"My pleasure. I'll see you Monday at six?"

"Yes, I'll be here to set up and, of course, you're welcome to join us."

"Thank you, Lily, and I just might. I've always been a fan of mystery movies."

With that settled, I checked my watch and said I needed to leave, but I'd see her Monday.

"By the way, did you get a package from Flora?"

I paused. "A package?"

"Yes, there was something she wanted delivered to you so she hired a messenger service the day"—her hands flew to her throat—"you know. She died."

"Oh, yes, I got it and thanks for clearing up how it was delivered. I thought it was odd."

Her face scrunched up, and then it relaxed. "Oh, right. It came the same day, didn't it?"

"Yes. I need to run but see you Monday." When I got to the door, I felt like I was being watched. I turned and Meredith waved to me. I returned the gesture and was on my way.

Later that afternoon, I had my book, *Practical Beginnings*, open. It was no longer sending up choking billows of dust. It was open in front of me, but I couldn't concentrate on the words. Instead, I kept glancing at the screen on my phone. Specifically, the photo I had taken of the murder board last night before I put it in the pantry. I needed to change the way I referred to my chalkboard. It was a clue magnet. That sounded infinitely better in my mind.

Milo was snoozing in a sun-filled window, stretched as long as he was able. I had checked in with Aunt Mimi and she was doing fine and lobster was still on tonight's menu. I planned on running by her place on my way home. Nate said he'd bring it to their place and save me a trip to the docks.

I couldn't get my mind off Teddy and the mystery man. How was I going to finagle a one-on-one with the first and discover the identity of the second? I snapped the book closed and picked up my duster. Maybe a mindless task would help me focus. I hadn't been at it long when the bell on the door dinged, announcing a customer. I walked around the end of the aisle and a tall and very thin man was standing in the doorway. He had closely cropped hair that reminded me of a military buzz, no facial hair, but a wide scar above his left eye. He didn't venture in any farther and looked decidedly uncomfortable.

He should either come in or go out. I kept my voice warm and upbeat despite the odd behavior. "Welcome to The Cozy Nook Bookshop. Is there anything special I can help you find?"

"Just the owner." His voice had a noticeable Southern drawl.

I took a step closer to him and flashed what I hoped was my most friendly smile. Based on his severely tailored jacket, crisp blue shirt, and distressed and pressed jeans, he wasn't a local. Besides that, I knew almost everyone in this small town and who ironed their jeans?

"I'm Lily Michaels. The owner. How may I help you?"

He frowned and looked around as if he didn't believe me. "I was looking for an older woman, closer to seventy."

"That would be my aunt. She sold the shop to me a few years ago." So that explained it, a former customer coming back to see Aunt Mimi. "I'd be happy to help you. Are you looking for a specific title, perhaps a collector's copy of something or a new bestseller?"

He took a step inside. As he drew closer, a shiver raced down my spine. I moved closer to the desk where I had left my cell phone. Darn Milo was still sleeping and just when I might need backup. Wait, a cat wasn't going to help. It wasn't like he could do magic or anything. Best he could do would be to scratch the man.

"I understand Ms. Michaels was questioned about the death of Flora Gray."

I didn't respond, but slowly slipped my hand

over my phone and wondered if I could get a phone call off to Gage before this guy lunged at me.

I wished Gage were striding through the door right now. I glanced at the glass and dark wood, but someone definitely shut it tight.

"You know she had nothing to do with it."

His eyes locked on mine. My heart ticked up. The blood roared in my ears and my mouth was dry like the sand at the beach after a midsummer day. I couldn't speak. All I wanted was for Gage to walk in that door. I closed my eyes for a moment and really concentrated, asking him to come to the shop. When I opened them, the man was directly in front of me.

"Do you know who I am?"

I shook my head and managed to eek out, "No."

"Good. All you need to know is I have a few friends in this town and Mimi used to be one of them. Tell your buddy, that detective, she had nothing to do with it and to find someone else to harass."

"Why don't you tell me yourself instead of harassing the lady?"

At the sound of Gage's voice, relief washed over me. I was no longer alone. Not that I couldn't have handled the situation given a bit more time to think, but now I didn't have to.

The man whirled around and faced Gage. "I can vouch for Ms. Michaels. I saw Flora Gray lying face-first on the stairs before Mimi came out of the library. She stopped the bat from falling on Flora and screamed for help. A few moments later, this lady ran out and checked Flora's pulse. Of course, she was already dead."

"Are you giving me an official statement, Mr....?"

"Dax Peters."

"And why are you coming forward now?" Gage planted his feet the same width as his shoulders, appearing cool and confident. Every inch my hero.

"I'm not always quick to do the right thing, but I didn't want an innocent woman to be questioned again."

"Then why didn't you come forward that night?"

Good question. As far as I was concerned, Gage was doing a good job following up with Dax Peters. I anxiously awaited the answers, too.

"To be candid, I thought you would have arrested someone by now, the real murderer."

"We're investigating and we don't make a habit of running around arresting people before we have solid evidence. Where are you staying?" Gage had a notepad out and jotted something down. He looked at Peters expectantly.

"At the Coastal Motel on Route 1A. Room 110. I'll be leaving next week." He reached into his jacket pocket, then thrust a business card at Gage.

He read it, then looked up at Peters and gave a curt nod.

"You need to work a little harder to wrap up your investigation and have this one"—he jerked his thumb in my direction—"stop snooping around. I hear things and the actual killer is going to get annoyed. I'd hate for anything to happen to a nice lady and one who is Mimi's niece."

"Are you threatening me?" I walked around the desk and stepped between Gage and Mr. Peters.

"No. I'm trying to look out for your health." He gave a curt nod to us both and strode out the door, closing it with a firm *thud*.

I whirled around. "Why didn't you stop him?"

He held up the business card. "I need to check him out, but I'm sure he's not a suspect."

If Gage was sure, then I wouldn't waste time thinking about Dax. I trusted Gage with my life. But I wanted to keep him from reminding me to stay out of the investigation. Changing the subject was the best way to do that. Flashing him a wide smile, I said, "This is a surprise. Why did you stop in?"

He scratched his head. "I don't think you'd believe me if I told you."

Now that was an odd way for him to answer

my question. "Try me." I placed my hand on his arm, instantly drawing in his strength.

"I was getting ready to drive out to Marshall Stone's farm and it was like I heard your voice in my head asking me to stop. When I pulled out of the parking lot, it was as if my car had a mind of its own or I just wasn't that concerned with questioning Marshall and here I am."

I withdrew my hand. Had I summoned Gage to me, like I had done with Aunt Mimi? "I'm glad you stopped by. I was a little nervous with Mr. Peters." I happened to glance at Milo, who was sitting up in the window, watching everything as it unfolded. How long he had been paying attention was anyone's guess. But the only explanation for Gage coming was I did it. This was something Milo and I would talk about later.

"I need to take off and get out to the farm, but we're still on for dinner tonight?"

"Yes, but Marshall's not your guy." It was then I realized what I had said. I instantly regretted my comment since I wasn't planning on telling Gage what I had learned at the farm until I knew more.

"Lily."

The sharp and questioning warning tone came through loud and clear. I gave him my *I'm innocent* look, but his frown was deep. "What did you do this time?"

Once again, I tried to feign innocence, but his scowl said he wasn't buying it. I should tell him everything. Maybe it would help him with his questions. "Nikki and I went out to the farm stand as I told you last night. While I was chatting with Marshall, I mentioned Jill was in and planning a trip. I thought he might be going with her, but he said he never leaves the county, much less the state."

"That proves nothing." He crossed his arms over his chest and leaned against the counter. If this was his attempt to appear casual, it wasn't working. His body was taut and ready for action.

"I know that doesn't, but he was genuinely sorry Flora was dead and unless he was an actor, no one could fake that."

"Killers can be consummate actors. I can rattle off a list of them."

"But this was an act of impulse. Using a baseball bat in such a public forum. Unless the person had been thinking about killing her and this was the best opportunity they'd had." If that were true, then it was risky with so many people around. "Or it had to be in a fit of rage. Flora pushed one too many buttons." I waved my hand. "I've gotten off the subject of Marshall. He has a thing for Jill Dilly. Did you know that? But she is interested in someone else. If he was going to do anything to anyone, it would be his rival. Not the poor blackmailing librarian."

He laughed. "Poor librarian, who happens to be a blackmailer. That is an oxymoron."

I laughed too. Gage had a way of putting things into perspective. "There probably isn't anyone who feels sorry for her. I mean, getting clonked over the head had to have hurt." I winced just thinking about it.

"If it makes you feel any better, she probably

didn't know what hit her. She died almost instantly."

I made a *tsk tsk* sound and then said, "Gallows humor, really? And from a detective."

"Now that we know I can be a little callous, which in my line of work is a good thing, tell me why else you think Marshall is innocent."

I thought back to the way he looked and reacted while we were talking about Flora and his friends. "Part intuition and the other just observation. He's a gentle giant and there's no way he could have been the one."

"Do you remember where he was when your aunt screamed?"

I closed my eyes and rewound that night. "He was getting the projector ready. I remember he was talking about Flora being cantankerous and the next thing was Aunt Mimi screaming for help."

"What about before that?" He continued to push me to really think back to where everyone was. "Where were Jill and Teddy?"

"There were a bunch of people milling

around taking seats, but I can't say for sure. After Flora flounced out of the room, we just wanted to watch the movie. I couldn't pinpoint anyone else."

"Alright, I'll see you later at your place and please try to keep your focus on the shop. If you feel we must continue to talk about this case, we can do so at home."

I could see the twinkle in his eyes and knew he wasn't really mad at me. "See you later."

Gage gave me a friendly hug. "Stay out of mischief for the rest of the day. Please?"

Flashing him a sweet smile, I promised I'd do my best. What he didn't see was my fingers crossed behind my back.

Chapter 17
Gage

When I got to Lily's place, the house was lit up and jazz music was spilling out of the speakers on her back deck. It was a warm night and eating outside was a great idea, especially given that we were going to be shucking lobsters. I tapped on the back door and walked in. There was a tray with plates, oversized paper napkins, silverware, and of course, lobster crackers, along with a tossed salad. But what drew my attention was the pie resting on the counter. Nikki had baked it, and I was already looking forward to a large slice with ice cream.

"Lily, I'm here," I called out, wondering what she was doing.

"Be right there." Her voice came from the end of the hallway.

A minute later, she came in lugging the chalkboard easel she had set up the other night as her murder board. She leaned it against the far wall and inwardly, I sighed. There was no escaping her desire to solve this case. Part of me understood since Mimi was in the crosshairs. I had been hoping tonight would have been about us and maybe for the first time she'd see me as more than her BFF.

Her cheeks were flushed and her soft brown eyes sparkled with mischief. It looked as if she had just gotten out of the shower as her pixie-brown hair was slightly damp. "Hey there. Right on time."

"Punctuality is my middle name." I laughed, remembering how she always teased me as kids when I couldn't be late for class. Maybe that's why I became a cop. There was some unpredictability in the job, along with order.

"I had a slight detour after work." She grabbed my hand and pulled me to the deck. "Let's sit down and have a glass of wine. I'll tell you all about it."

I gave her a long look. She was up to something. I knew it. "Maybe I should have a beer."

Her laughter confirmed my suspicion. Something was going on, and I guess she had been doing her version of investigating. Lily went back into the kitchen for my beer, and I took a seat in one of the cushioned chairs and propped my feet on the footstool. I wanted to be comfortable with whatever was going to come next.

When she came back, she was carrying a tray with assorted appetizers and a frosty mug filled to the rim. "Here we go. Might as well relax. We've got all evening to enjoy dinner."

I exhaled. Maybe I'd been wrong, and we were just going to have a nice evening together. Or maybe she was ready for me to open up and share how I really felt about her.

Holding up her glass, she tapped my beer mug. "To Nate."

Huh. That was not what I had been expecting. I must have been wearing a weird expression since she started laughing.

"Wait until you see the lobsters we have. I'll steam both of them, but we have enough for dinner, breakfast, and lunch. They're huge."

"Good day on the boat." I took a long drink of my beer and now I knew she was stalling. Small talk and that glint in her eye never went together. She knew something. Now to find out what.

"What time did you close the shop?" I took a cracker and a sliver of cheese.

"Around four. There were a couple of things I wanted to do before I had to swing by my aunt's house."

I waited for her to continue, but she grinned like a Cheshire cat. Finally, she said, "Aren't you going to ask me what they were?"

"You're dying to tell me. Go for it." I wished I had my notebook to jot down whatever she said, but if there was anything worthwhile, I could have her tell the story again.

She scooted her chair closer and rubbed her hands together. "After you left the shop, I went and talked to Teddy. So now, three of the four suspects from Teddy's get-together have shared details of that night."

"You did what?" I gripped the handle on the mug a little tighter. "That could have been dangerous, especially going there alone."

"I wasn't. Milo came with me."

I hung my head. Lily exhausted me with her odd logic. "Milo doesn't have the ability to help if things went south with Teddy. He could be the killer."

Her confident smile gave me a chill down my spine. It was obvious she had taken an enormous risk earlier, and I needed to know what had happened, but a part of me was afraid to probe deeper. "Alright. What was said? And I want all the details." I put extra emphasis on *all* to encourage her to tell me everything. "It's better I know in case I had to bat cleanup."

She smiled. "Is that a direct reference to the crime you're dealing with?"

I cringed. "A poor baseball metaphor, but Lily, just tell me what happened and don't leave anything out."

"Alright. Sheesh. Give a girl a break."

She didn't sound upset or annoyed, which helped lessen the hard rock that had formed in my gut.

"After you left, I wondered if Teddy has a romantic interest in Jill. Could there be a love triangle at play between Jill, Marshall, and Teddy? Was this why they each were being blackmailed by Flora? Marshall's unrequited love, Jill's passion for Teddy, and potentially his indifference to them both." She took a breath and tapped the tabletop. "I'm convinced the killer is Teddy. You can arrest him now." With a triumphant look, she leaned back in her chair.

I hadn't heard why she thought it was Teddy. Sipping my beer, I waited for her to expand on her announcement.

Tipping her head to one side, she said, "What?"

"We need a little thing called proof."

"I'll be right back." Lily jumped up and hurried into the house.

She was on fire tonight. Even though I had Teddy on my list, the information I had was thin. Mimi was still the best suspect on paper, even though in my mind she had been cleared.

A clattering sound caught my attention and Milo had pushed through the lightweight screen door ahead of her. If I didn't know better, I would have thought he was holding it for her. I got up and took the board. I leaned it against a chair and saw she had written more notes since the last time I was here.

"Walk me through what you think happened." I knew she had a sharp mind, but what I wasn't sure of was if she was analytical enough to decipher the noise from what was important.

"You can ask questions, but don't downplay any of my ideas, okay?"

I nodded and gave her an encouraging smile. "Take your time. I have all night."

With a tentative smile, she said, "Almost one week ago we know that Flora Gray was murdered. She was blackmailing or attempting to blackmail ten or more citizens in Pembroke. What secret she had on each person is currently unknown. Either no one is talking and she didn't write it down or she wrote it down and I'm not privy to it." She gave me a questioning look.

"We've found nothing other than what you've seen by your foray into the library." I liked how she was starting her impromptu presentation but wanted to point out that she had jumped ahead of our investigation.

"The top four suspects are Aunt Mimi, Jill Dilly, Marshall Stone, and Teddy Roberts. Out of the four, three had paid some amount of money to keep their secret quiet. Aunt Mimi wasn't giving in and this gave her a powerful motive. But what if the remaining three were working together? That night, they all came and left the library together, which is something I had never seen before. Marshall had brought Jill twice, but he drove past her house on the way into town, so that makes sense. But Teddy lives in the opposite direction, so to pick him up was out of the way."

I tipped my head and saw how she was laying this out, and I was curious to see where she was going.

"Marshall was setting up the movie when Aunt Mimi screamed. But as you know, I can't recall seeing Jill and Teddy after I got there. I talked with Flora, who was her usual cranky self, about me cleaning up after the movie was over. Meredith walked over and reminded Flora we always left the space immaculate. But Flora, being *ever gracious*, glared at Meredith, who slipped away." She paced a bit. "I ran outside after I heard the scream and Mimi was holding the bat and the look of horror on her face is one I'll never forget. It was not of a woman who had just committed murder. And Dax Peters confirmed Flora was already dead." She frowned. "Not that I'm sure we can rely on his word."

"We can. He's in law enforcement."

"That's what he says."

"Lily, I checked him out and his story matches up. He's one of the good guys."

Her eyes narrowed. "Then why is he in town?"

"I'm not in the loop on that case, at least not yet." I pointed to her board. "Continue."

"Oh. Right. After I confirmed she was dead, I remember looking around the group that had followed me out. Jill, Teddy, and Marshall were all standing huddled together. Teddy had a smug smile on his face. Jill didn't look shocked, but Marshall seemed stunned."

She waited to see if I had a comment. "You're saying because Teddy looked almost happy it had to be him?"

She snapped her fingers and pointed her index finger at me. "Yes. He was strong enough to swing the bat and send her flying face-first down the stairs. He was paying her off. With her dead, the drain on his savings ended, and when I saw him today, he actually said he was relieved

251

the old biddy was out of his hair. His words, not mine." She gave me a small smile.

"That doesn't mean he's a killer."

"What about that he hasn't seen or talked to Marshall or Jill since right after the murder and he said he's going out of town? Is that a coincidence since Jill is planning a trip, too? Love triangle. Marshall drove the getaway car, literally, with Jill and Teddy giving each other an alibi. Oh, and I saw him stuffing something in his pocket. When I asked him about it today, he said it was his handkerchief and he'd had a nosebleed. I'll bet it had Flora's blood on it. He had to clean up somehow, right?"

This was the first I had heard Teddy had a supposed nosebleed, but I kept my face neutral so Lily wouldn't go down that rabbit hole. She was already standing on the edge. "This is great work. How did you leave it with Teddy? Please tell me you didn't accuse him of the murder?"

"Of course not. I asked when he was going on his trip and if he was going alone."

I suppressed a laugh. She was like a shark

with fish, never giving up until she extracted everything she wanted. "And he said?"

"He was going away with his lady friend next week. You'll need to finish putting the case together so you can arrest him on Monday night."

"I'll bet you asked if he was coming?"

She crossed her arms over her midsection. "Gage, what kind of sleuth would I be if I hadn't?" She pointed to the last item on the board. Where it said in all caps: TRIO WILL ATTEND.

I had to admit it was solid even without access to our interviews. "You would have made a decent cop."

She beamed at my compliment. "Thanks. Are you ready for dinner? And then you can go arrest him."

"Yes, to dinner and no, I can't arrest him tonight. We didn't find his fingerprints on the weapon. He didn't have blood on his clothes, and there would have been some additional evidence based on how hard she had to have been struck.

Just because he had a bloody handkerchief doesn't mean he's guilty. Also, going on vacation with your girlfriend isn't a crime. But I will look at everything again." I pointed to the board. "But take a picture of this and put it away."

Her brows knitted together. "Why do you suppose she had those roses underneath her body?"

"Our best guess is she found them on the steps or something and picked them up. I don't think they have to do with the case."

"And the candy wrapper?"

Dang, her mind was razor-sharp. "Someone missed the trash can, nothing noteworthy."

She nodded. "You're probably right. I just wish I could dismiss the flowers. The colors are for love, friendship, and purity. Again, the number three." She folded the board. "I'll drop the lobsters in the pot. Care to help?"

I said, "Yes." As we walked inside, I could see the pattern now that Lily pointed it out and it needed more thought.

Chapter 18
Lily

I was glad Saturday was in the rearview mirror. The shop had been insane with customers, and I had zero time to check in with Gage about the investigation. Now that it was finally Sunday, and in my opinion the best day of the week, I could relax. I always had breakfast with Aunt Mimi and Nate. Sometimes, if I got lucky, she'd make her legendary Belgian waffles and thick slab bacon. But today I was bringing over the big book and Milo was going with me. She was going to help me work on the next spell and practice the first three I had sort of learned. I dressed quickly, called to Milo that we needed to hurry, and when he didn't appear, I went looking for him.

"Milo? Where are you hiding?" I searched the house and opened the back door, only to discover him stretched out in the morning sun across the bistro table. I scratched between his ears to wake him up.

"I'm sleeping." If a cat could growl, Milo had perfected it.

"It's time to go to Aunt Mimi's and I'll bet she'll give you some bacon." I was not above bribing him. I enjoyed having him around as I was working on spells. He was my good luck charm.

He rolled over on his back and batted at me with his paw, with claws in. Evidently, he was feeling frisky this morning. "I'm not riding in that carrier. It's too confining now that I got to ride sitting on a seat."

I popped my hands on my hips. "I want to do it for safety. In case I got into an accident or something, you wouldn't be flying all over the car."

He looked at me with slitted eyes. "Since you know I'm magically inclined, I'm pretty sure I can hold my own in a car."

Now I was getting peeved. "In my defense, when I bought the cat carrier, I did not know about your never-ending abilities."

With a languid stretch, he finally got to all four paws, stalked across the table, and jumped down. "I'm ready. Let's roll."

Only I would have a sarcastic familiar. Or maybe that was something else I should talk to Aunt Mimi and Nikki about. It could be a trait of all familiars. I grabbed my bag and locked the back door before hurrying to the car, skipping the carrier and letting Milo hop in first and get comfy on the passenger seat.

The drive was over in minutes and Nate was standing on the top step of the kitchen. He must have been watching for me since the door opened the minute I drove up the driveway. I waved and followed Milo up the short brick walk. The house was an old, weathered cottage; additions sprung up from each side over the last few generations. Aunt Mimi liked it since it was the only home facing the ocean with a widow's walk. Not that she spent time watching for Nate's lobster boat, but she always said she liked being close to nature, even during the most ferocious storms.

Another piece of the puzzle clicked into place. Maybe Aunt Mimi was a green witch, one in touch with nature, but wait, that was all about growing things. I tried to remember what I had read about the different types of witches, but it escaped me what else she might be. I could ask her over breakfast since Nate knew all about the woman he had loved for decades. The entire family never understood why she hadn't married him, but as long as they were happy, I didn't care if there was a license and a ring or not.

Milo trotted over to Aunt Mimi, who had a crumble of bacon in her outstretched hand. "Good morning, Milo."

He delicately took the treat and hopped up

on the overstuffed reading chair next to the bay window. For the first time, I realized just how many windows this house had. Phoenix, a black cat with just a tiny tuft of white on her chest, strolled into the kitchen. Looking from me to Milo, she hopped up next to my kitty.

"Hello, Phoenix." I bent to kiss the top of her head and she purred, a loud motorboat rumble.

"Lily. It's nice to finally talk to you."

My head snapped toward my aunt. "She really is your familiar?"

"Yes. You know Phoenix came to me years ago and we've been tight ever since."

That showed Milo would be with me for maybe the rest of my life. "It's just that Phoenix has never talked to me before."

"And why would she? You hadn't tapped into your magic yet. Now that you have, you'll have the ability to talk to Phoenix and Nikki's familiar, too."

Nate held up the coffeepot and mug. "Ready for a dose of the good stuff?"

Was I ever. I held out my hand, and he put

the mug of steaming coffee in it as I made my way to the table. It was all part of our practiced routine.

I didn't offer to help, not that I was being rude, but I was never allowed to lift a finger. Aunt Mimi liked to play the hostess of the hour and I was happy to let her. I returned the gracious gesture when she and Nate came to my place for dinner.

"Have you spoken with Gage about the investigation?" Nate sat next to me, trying his best to sound casual. But we knew it was more to do with Aunt Mimi being a suspect than idle conversation.

"Nate, you know we had dinner Friday night." I tried to keep my voice light and teasing, hoping to reassure him. "Thank you again for the lobsters. They were sweet and tender. A perfect way to end a not-so-great week."

He gave me a wide smile. "My pleasure, but seriously, what, if anything, did Gage say about Flora's untimely demise?"

"Good news. I'm fairly certain that I've

cracked the case for him. I'm sure he'll follow up on everything and by this time Tuesday morning, the killer or killers will be sitting in the Pembroke jail and Mimi will be one hundred percent cleared."

"That is very good news." Mimi sat down. "But how can you be so positive?"

I placed my hand over hers, hoping it comforted her. "I handed over all my evidence to Gage and I'm holding movie night tomorrow and there will be an arrest. Until that happens, I'd like to forget about everything today and concentrate on this delicious breakfast. After that, maybe we can talk about the spells I've learned. I'd really like to know what kind of witch you are and if you have any idea about me. Nikki told me she was a kitchen witch and since I struggle in that part of the house, I'm certain that's not me."

Nate grinned. "I think concentrating on something positive is what we all need today. In honor of all things witchy, I'll volunteer to clean up so you ladies can relax and do whatever you need to do."

Mimi leaned over the table and pecked his lips. "That is why I love you."

His face melted into a puddle of squishiness. "Mermaid, I love you too."

Somewhere in my core, I wished Gage would look at me like that over the breakfast table. Maybe there was a love spell I could try. As quickly as it came to mind, I dismissed it. If he was going to fall for me, it was the old-fashioned mortal way or not at all. I looked up and said to no one in particular, "How about a waffle drowning in maple syrup?"

With my belly full, I was ready to dive into all things witchy. "Aunt Mimi. Are you a green witch?"

Her coffee cup was halfway to her lips, and she paused. "No preamble, Lily?"

"Sorry. In my head, we've been having a conversation, and it just popped out." I didn't feel embarrassed about just blurting the question out, but she hadn't answered yet either.

"No. I'm not a green witch. That is someone who is a natural healer and is a fantastic gardener, growing what she needs for her craft. I'm a cosmic witch."

That wasn't a subset of witches that I had read about in my book. "What exactly does that mean?"

She gestured to the stairs. "Come with me."

I followed her up two sets of stairs and out onto the widow's walk.

She raised her hands, palms skyward. "Astronomy. The cycles of the moon are where I draw energy to help me cast my spells."

There was a finality in her voice and now was not the time to ask more questions. She turned to me. "You are an eclectic witch. You'll find you have many talents and can dabble in many areas."

I had read something about that branch. I figured it was the best way to describe the different witches. "Does this mean I will have to study forever?"

Her laughter was musical. "No. You're discovering your niche even if you don't realize it." She walked me to a bench along the banister. "Sit."

I did as she asked and looked out over the ocean. "I'd never tire of this view."

"We don't." She took a seat next to me and placed her hand over mine. "This week has been a lot for you. Trying to help me with Flora's murder, Milo, the big book, and Nikki. Most people deal with just one of these. Tell me how you're really handling everything."

"I'm good." But I could hear the waver in my voice and I was sure Aunt Mimi could, too. She waited. "I mean, I've thrown myself into making sure that Gage arrests the right person."

"That was his job, Lily, not yours."

I dipped my head. "It felt good to be actively helping my favorite aunt who is important to me."

"I'm your only aunt." She squeezed my hand. "Tell me about your summoning spell. I'm surmising you took the basics and somehow made it your own."

"I've been able to bring you and Gage to me. Milo made fun of my spell, but it worked. Do they have to be exact, like in the book? Memorizing them verbatim?"

"Magic is personal."

That was something I wanted to hear. "I'm comfortable with the summoning, lighting candles, and location spells. I don't think I need anything more."

Aunt Mimi got up and crossed to the railing. She had her back to me. "You need one more. A spell of protection."

Her voice was solemn and a shiver of fear ran down my spine. I have never had this feeling before and it made me want to get the book, find the spell, and practice it until it was perfect. "Let's get started."

Six hours later, I still hadn't mastered the spell. I threw my hands up and flopped on the sofa in Aunt Mimi's living room. "I give up."

"I'm tripping over the words, and my frustration is growing. Maybe this is one that needs to wait until another day."

Her mouth formed a hard line. "No. You need to find a way to make it work. Today."

I sat up straight and leaned forward, my arms resting on my jean-clad legs. "Why? What do you know?"

"I don't know anything specific, but I have a feeling and I've learned to trust them, just as you need to learn to trust your inner voice. There is a reason it talks to you. Listen to it." Aunt Mimi grabbed my hands and pulled me to a standing position. "Clear your mind and do it again."

I took several deep breaths and shook out my shoulders like a prizefighter getting ready for a big match. I closed my eyes and then peeked at her with one. "Who am I protecting?"

"It depends. You, a friend, a stranger, a loved one. It's intentional. Instinctive."

I had to laugh at how my aunt drawled out

the last three words. "Alright, I'll try again." I could feel Aunt Mimi watching me closely. I thought of why she might need protection. The worry of her being arrested for a crime she didn't commit swept over me.

"From the depth of my soul to the recess of my brain. I wrap Aunt Mimi in the protection of my love." The energy flowed through my body and I projected it onto her. I heard her draw in a deep breath.

"That's it, Lily. Push. Push yourself." Her voice was soft and reverent. Encouraging. Supportive.

I remained focused. In my mind's eye, I could see it surround her with a deep-purple haze. It suited her. When I knew it was strong enough, I opened my eyes.

Her face was all shiny, and her eyes were bright. "You did it."

"Does this mean you're protected from anything bad happening in conjunction with the investigation?"

"We shall see. But for now, know that you

can do the spell and it will work for you and those you care about."

I threw my arms around her. "Thank you for helping me." I looked around for Milo, but he wasn't anywhere to be seen.

"Don't worry about him. He and Phoenix went out a while ago. I think they're visiting with other familiars in town."

"How many of us are there here in Pembroke?"

"Let's have some tea. That conversation is for another day." She looped her arm through mine. "Tell me, what is your plan for tomorrow night?"

Back to the complex plan. "I'm going to get to the library around five and set up an area where we can expose the killers."

"You're convinced it's more than one person?"

I nodded. "I think there are several people working together on various levels. Tomorrow night Gage will be there and I'm going to go over my murder board and confront the guilty parties.

Once they confess, he can arrest them, and then we can get down to the real reason we're at the library. I want to see that movie." I grinned. Had my attempt to lighten the mood worked?

"Murder and the movies don't really go together."

Now I laughed. "Neither do books and blackmail, but here we are."

Chapter 19
Lily

I closed the bookshop early and took Milo home. I wasn't sure how late the night would be, so I changed into comfortable jeans, a deep-purple tee shirt, and sneakers for movie night. The night was planned. Nikki and her boyfriend Steve would meet me there at six. I had told everyone who was coming to watch the movie to be there at six thirty, but I wanted to get there at five. My intention was to walk through the scene of the crime again and talk to Meredith. She might have noticed someone following Flora out of the building and I was sure it was Teddy. The dollar amount next to his name had been the largest in the notebook. He had the most to gain by Flora's death—him and Jill.

"I'll see you later, Milo." I scratched the top of his head as I put out fresh water and, as a special treat, a can of fancy tuna.

He paced the floor in front of me. "Remember your spells. Now that you have magic, if anything goes sideways, use it."

I appreciated his concern, but nothing was going to go wrong. "You worry too much, my friend. Friends and family will surround me. No one will be able to hurt me."

"Except the murderer."

He really hadn't needed to point out there was still a killer roaming around town. But after tonight, all would be right with our quiet little town again. And there would be one, if not two, new residents in the town jail. "I'll see you later."

Milo swished his tail and it smacked my leg with a *thwoop*. "I have no plans to get a new witch, so be careful. Mind your spells and stay out of trouble."

"Stop nagging, fur bag."

He stalked out of the kitchen without even touching his dinner. I hadn't meant to hurt his feelings, and I didn't even know where the fur bag comment had come from. But I was annoyed he kept harping on me and it slipped out.

My alarm went off on my phone, reminding me I needed to get going. I didn't want anyone to notice me poking around while I firmed up my theory. It would be embarrassing to accuse an innocent person. I couldn't help but wonder if I was really certain or if, for lack of a better suspect, I was blaming Teddy much the way Gage had thought it was Aunt Mimi.

I got in my car and reviewed my evidence. Teddy was the only suspect that made sense, and Jill was his accomplice, with Marshall being the unwitting driver for the getaway car.

· · ·

Arriving at the library ten minutes later, I noticed the parking lot was virtually empty. It reminded me of last week, and I shook off the chill that raced down my arms. I was never a fan of déjà vu.

I jogged up the steps and pulled open the heavy wood and glass door, noticing to the right a vase of wildflowers with a mixture of roses. Had that been there last week? Is that where the roses under Flora's body had come from? I paused and turned to look at the spot where Flora had lain and then back at the vase. In my mind, I could see her stopping to select a few flowers before descending the stairs. I made a mental note to ask Meredith who put the flowers out there.

The interior of the library was cool and quiet, almost tomblike. My eyes adjusted from the bright sun to the dimly lit space. Down each aisle lined with books it was brighter, but the vestibule seemed darker, almost ominous. I shook off the gloom. Most days there was the pleasant chatter of children's voices that drifted out of the story corner, but today, like last week, it was devoid of kids. Adjusting my shoulder strap on my bag, I walked deeper into the building. I detoured through the book section where the deep-green carpet absorbed the sound of my steps. I didn't see Meredith or anyone else, so I went straight back to the community room. If anyone wondered why I was here early, I could say it was to get things set up or even that I was looking for a book. After all, this was the best place to get one.

I flicked on the overhead lights and there at the back of the room sat Meredith. The soft sound of hiccups reached me. I hurried over, dropping my bag in a chair.

I knelt next to her. "Hey, Meredith. What's going on?"

She looked up at me, her face stained with tears and her eyes bloodshot from crying. "I can't believe she's dead. That she's never coming back. I keep thinking it's a dream and Flora is going to walk through the front door, barking orders, being rude to everyone, and getting into everyone's business. Just like she always did."

I took her hand, and it was ice-cold. In an attempt to get some warmth back into it, I massaged her skin, but to no avail. "Let's go wash your face before people come in for the movie." I really wanted to retrace Flora's steps that I knew, but that would have to wait.

"I guess Flora's death has hit you pretty hard?" I helped Meredith up from the chair and slipped my arm around her waist and we made our way to the staff break area in the back room.

She gave me a smile of thanks. "You've been so nice to everyone here. I'm sorry Flora always gave you a hard time about your mystery night. I knew you never left a mess. She just liked to complain. I think it was the only thing that made her happy." She took a piece of paper towel and dampened it. "That and money."

What had she just said? No one knew she had money. Could Meredith be referring to her cache?

"Flora wanted to retire and said that given one more year, she'd be set for life." Meredith pressed the towel to her flushed cheeks and red-rimmed eyes.

"I didn't know she was a good investor."

She swung around from the sink after tossing the towel. "She had a way of getting what she needed."

Was it my imagination or had her tone sharpened? "I'm glad she was looking forward to her future."

I wanted to get out of the small room, so I eased toward the door. "You know I'm curious if there were any kids from Little League in the library the day Flora died."

"No. I remember one of the moms stopping in to pick up Jane Austen. She said it was like watching paint dry at the game sometimes, so she needed new reading material."

Before I could stop myself, I let slip, "I wonder where the baseball bat came from then. If there weren't any kids around to have left it." I knew I was starting to prattle but what did it matter. I was pretty sure I was about to be shocked.

"It was in the lost and found for ages. Anyone could have seen it." She took a sip of water from a bottle on the counter. "I think like a month or more."

That was way too quick of an answer. I eased out of the room and took a deep breath of air. Just being in the wide, open room made me feel better. "I'm just going to check the projector. But I'll see you later?"

"I'm not going anywhere." She watched me closely, and it unnerved me.

What was going on behind those wire-rimmed glasses? Meredith appeared to be a mouse, but I was beginning to think she might be hiding very sharp teeth. I needed to text Gage to have him check a few things before coming over. Yesterday, Aunt Mimi had told me to listen to my inner voice. Right now, she was screaming at me, full volume.

I took a deep breath and gave her a forced smile. Hopefully, she wouldn't guess I was uncomfortable with our current situation. "I hope you're going to join us for the movie." I had asked her this question every time, and she always said no. But hey, I tried.

"I've been looking forward to it since you mentioned it on Friday. It's been a long time since I watched a good flick. It's even better that it's a mystery."

I nodded, turned, and forced myself to take my time walking to the room. All the while, my heart was pounding and my blood was roaring. I had to get to Gage, and fast.

Over my shoulder, Meredith called out, "Thanks again for asking me."

I flashed her a wide smile and tapped my watch. "I'll be back shortly."

Once safely in the room, I pushed the door closed and withdrew my phone from my back pocket. I hesitated. Should I text? Calling was more efficient than trying to type out my questions. I called him and thankfully he answered on the second ring.

I glanced at the door, satisfied I was alone. I cupped a hand over my mouth and the receiver and turned away from the room entrance, moving closer to an outer wall. "Gage. It's me, Lily."

"Hi. You didn't change the time of the movie, did you? Or have your suspects decided not to come and I need to change my plan?"

I usually found it endearing when he tried to guess why I was calling, but not tonight. "Shush," I demanded. "You need to check on a few things before you come over tonight. I think I might have pointed you in the wrong direction. I need for you to check on Meredith Poole. When I got to the library, she was sobbing and talking about Flora. Meredith said something about Flora's retirement fund and she confirmed the bat came from the lost and found."

"That's hardly proof. Besides, her name wasn't on the blackmail list." He let out a low whistle. "Back up. Rewind. Did you say you're already at the library?"

"Yes. I came early to walk through the crime scene one more time. This thing with the flowers is bugging me."

"I want you to walk out of the building. Tell

Meredith you forgot something and go wait in your car until I get there. She might be harmless as a butterfly, but I don't want you to take the chance."

I nodded. My mouth had gone dry.

"Lily. Did you hear me?"

"Yes. I'll meet you outside." I picked up my shoulder bag and heard Gage say he would be here soon.

I slid the phone back into my pocket and opened the door. I ran into Meredith standing on the other side. Had she been listening to my conversation?

"Hey. I just need to run out to my car, but I'll be right back in."

She narrowed her eyes. "I'll walk you to the door. But you know, I was thinking about Flora that night."

I waited while she unwrapped a butterscotch candy and popped it into her mouth. "She and Teddy were arguing. I remember him saying the grapes wouldn't have much juice this year and she was going to be out of luck. Maybe she needed to think about another source. At the time I didn't think anything about it since he grows grapes and Marshall Stone does too, but now I'm not so sure. Maybe it was code for something more sinister."

The last word she said came out with an emphasis on the S like a snake.

"You should tell Gage when he gets here." I took a step, and she looped her arm through mine.

"I've always fancied myself like Jessica Fletcher, except I don't write mystery stories. I just manage the books here and read them."

I forced myself to smile and willed my heart to keep a steady beat. There was no sense in freaking out now. All she was doing was talking.

"Wouldn't it be fun if we pretended you're Flora and I'm the murderer?"

I swiveled my head and gave her a sharp look. "No. Things didn't turn out so great for Flora."

Her laugh was high and unnatural. "Not the full reenactment, but just up to when she's ready to walk out the door. With our two heads to-gether, I'll bet we can solve the mystery once and for all." She hugged my arm to her body tighter. "Wouldn't that be a hoot?"

I didn't like where this conversation was headed. When was Gage going to arrive? I needed backup, but for now, I needed to play along.

Meredith steered me in the direction of the desk Flora and she had been near the last time I talked with them. Before Flora left the building.

She pulled a stool over and placed it next to the desk. "I was standing right there." She put me in position. "And this is where Flora—now you—stood." She placed a hand over her heart. "And as for the murderer, I'm somewhere in the room watching everything." She frowned. "It's too bad we didn't have another person to play you. After all, Flora was horrible to you as usual that night."

"It's alright. I know what she said to me."

Meredith shook her head. "Authenticity is so

important when reenacting scenes. After all, the sleuth always does it in the movies."

Her voice was on the edge of crazy and not in a funny way. I scanned the room, wondering when people would need to check out books or where the other librarian was working. "Don't we need someone to represent you? I can call Nikki and she'll come down to help us." The rest of my thought died before it ever reached my lips.

Her lips had thinned, and her eyes narrowed. "I don't like Nikki. She thinks she's so pretty with those ocean-blue eyes and strawberry-blond hair. No."

That last word came out like a bark slash growl. Something inside caused her maniacal laughter to bubble to the surface. And as fast as it started, it died.

"Flora was mean. Did you know she was putting the squeeze on people? Bleeding them dry." She shook her head; her eyes were filled with disgust.

"You knew she was blackmailing people? How? Did she tell you?"

"Please. She never even gave me a second glance. Add in the years we worked together, she barely tolerated me. She always called me half-witted, stupid, and a small-town hick."

It finally clicked. Meredith killed Flora. But why go through the events again? Did she want to relive the thrill of the kill?

I moved away from my position behind the desk. Meredith didn't seem to notice. Lost in her own world of years of insults and belittling. "Why didn't you find a new job? One where you felt appreciated."

She threw back her head and snorted before leveling her gaze with mine. "I was not about to let her destroy my dream. When I was a little girl, my grandmother used to bring me here for story hour every Saturday morning. Those are my most treasured memories. Even then, I knew this was the only place I wanted to be. I was not about to let some bully shove me out. I deserved to be head librarian and knew if I waited patiently, Flora would retire and I'd be given the job I deserved." She paced the length of the space in front of the desk, wringing her hands. She wasn't looking at me now.

Knowing this was my only chance to do something proactive, I reached around to my back pocket and somehow snuck a peek at the screen and hit the audio record button and slipped it back into my jeans, hoping it would stay on and record the confession I planned to extract.

"Meredith. Why did you kill Flora?"

Chapter 20
Lily

Meredith looked at me with hatred; she was seeing someone else. "You have to die. All these years you've put me down and look at how you treated members of our community. Like they were your personal banks. Digging up dirt on people for mistakes anyone could make and then demanding money to keep their secrets. Poor Marshall. Having that terrible scar on his leg. When Jill asked him to go to the beach with her and he refused. He lost his chance with her. And then you seized upon his misfortune and promised to expose his feelings and what you called his deformity, not just to Jill but the whole town. Said you had pictures to back up your story. Such a sweet man and you were just horrid to him."

That confirmed part of what I already knew. Marshall cared for Jill. Meredith took a step closer to the desk, her hands forming fists by her sides. I wanted to tell her I wasn't Flora, but I also needed to know the rest of the story.

"You didn't stop with Marshall either. Teddy. Jill and then Mimi and Nate, plus a dozen more who either let you blab about their personal lives or paid you off. You're a despicable human being. Someone had to stop you from extracting every cent you could from good hardworking folks, and Mimi was trying. She wouldn't pay and you got angry." Her voice got louder, and she took another step in my direction. "I hated you, putting me down. Your cruelty to our neighbors was disgraceful."

"Just because Mimi said no to paying me

didn't mean I would have hurt her." I hoped I was playing Flora's part convincingly and this was an Oscar-worthy performance.

"I saw that look in your eye when you had that argument. Like always, I was invisible to you. When you picked up your things and without so much as good night you strode to the doors, I knew for the good of everyone in Pembroke you had to be stopped. I grabbed the bat I had stored in the closet and followed you." She pointed to the door. "Let's go."

"Meredith, it's me, Lily Michaels. I'm not Flora."

She blinked hard and shook her head, as if trying to clear her vision. I took that moment to run. But instead of running to the doors like she had wanted, I zipped down the fiction aisle. I dashed over to history. At the end of the aisle, I leaned against the wooden bookcase, doing my best to control my breathing. If she couldn't find me, there was time for Gage to arrive. Where was he? I needed him.

Silently, I groaned, remembering Milo's

words. Barely whispering, I said, "Gage, I summon you to me. I'm in trouble. Hurry." If there was one thing I knew about magic, words needed to be said, not thought. I repeated myself a little louder this time, and that was a mistake. Books came crashing down in back of me. I turned to my right and was on the move again.

"Flora, I know this building better than you. There is no place you can hide that I won't find you. Come out now and let's end this. I promise it will be quick. I've been practicing."

A shudder raced over me. How did you practice killing someone? I wanted to ask, but not really. "Milo. Please come. Milo, please come to me in the library." This time it wasn't books, but stacks of magazines crashed to the floor.

"I'm making a mess of this beautiful library. Which means I'll have to pick it up before everyone arrives for movie night, so just come out so we can finish our business." Her laugh was now full-on hysterical. "I mean, finish you."

Milo had said before I left, use my magic. Would the protection spell work on me? Before

I could concentrate, a baseball bat came crashing down on the table very close to where I was hiding. I jumped out of the corner and fled. By now I was so turned around that I didn't know where in the library I was. An exit sign glowed in the opposite direction. Hoping it was the front door, I made a run for it, only to trip over my shoelace and tumble head-first into kid-sized chairs. The children's section. Now I knew where I was and how to get out. Around me was silence. Meredith was no longer talking to Flora, me, or herself. That was not a good sign.

I crept down the aisle, keeping low, and when I came to the end, what I saw made my heart stop. Gage was walking in the door. He was completely unaware of what had happened since we talked, which seemed like a month ago. I waved in his direction, but he didn't see me.

I needed to protect him. Standing tall, I looked around and didn't see Meredith. I only had a few minutes to wrap the spell around Gage and protect him from anything Meredith might do. Silently, I said, *please let my magic be strong enough.*

I shook my arms to loosen the tension and, with my palms facing the sky, I closed my eyes. Concentrating harder than I had at Mimi's house, I spoke. "Protect Gage from all harm. Wrap around his body and mind so nothing can penetrate my spell. Keep him safe and well. Wrap him in the protection of my love." I repeated myself two more times, each time pushing myself to go deeper. With each word I spoke, I could feel my magic flowing across the room. When I opened my eyes, a transparent white bubble surrounded Gage. It took a second to realize it was different from Mimi's, but now was not the time to wonder why. All that mattered was Gage being safe.

Fingers tightened around my upper arm and I turned. Meredith had me in her clutches and began dragging me to the door. Her steps were silent. Gage still hadn't seen us. I wanted to call out, but she clamped her free hand over my mouth. I tried to bite her but to no avail. Her grip was like super glue. Yes, here I was about to die comparing things to hardware store purchases. Struggling, I knocked a chair over and finally, Gage saw me and I could see the fear in his eyes. If he didn't move soon, it was going to be too late. The only consolation I had was hope her confession was recorded.

He shouted, "Meredith. Stop!"

Her steps didn't slow, and I continued to fight against her. When had she gotten so strong? When we got close to the entrance, she barely paused, pulled her hand from my mouth, and shoved me out the door. It was then I caught sight of the silver and blue bat. It looked just like the one Aunt Mimi held in her hands just last week.

"Meredith, please. Don't. I'm not Flora. I'm Lily."

"I know who you are. Just like that old woman, you too have to die. I have to protect our community. Like her, you're a busybody. Having to know all the secrets. I won't let you hurt them."

Poised on the top step, I watched in horror. As if in slow motion, she raised the bat with two hands and swung like she was swinging for the cheap seats at Fenway. The scream didn't leave my lungs and I couldn't duck fast enough. My only choice was to throw myself down the steps and hope for the best. I took a giant leap from the top step but as I began to fall, the cement steps didn't rush up to greet me, and no pain flushed my body. Through a haze of pale yellow, I saw Aunt Mimi, her palms up, with Nikki beside her, doing the same.

I landed on the ground, and they rushed to my side. Nate was ready to help me up. Aunt Mimi was running her hands over my arms and legs, murmuring words I had never heard before. It was then that I looked at the top of the steps. Gage had Meredith's hands clasped in his behind her back. The bat lay on the ground without a drop of blood on it. I touched my head. Other than the little knot that remained from when I fell in the shop, it was injury free.

"How is that possible?" I looked around and

saw Milo trotting toward me. I scooped him up and gave him a long cuddle.

He began to purr and said, "Did you think after you summoned me I wouldn't call in rein-forcements?"

"Milo, I'm sorry for all the times this past week I was annoyed with you. You really are the best familiar ever."

"And someday I might say you're the best witch. But that's after a lot more lessons."

I hugged Milo to my chest as my grateful tears dampened his fur. Nate held out his strong and calloused hand to help me off the stone steps. Aunt Mimi and Nikki wrapped their arms around me with Milo still in my arms.

"I can't believe you came to help me."

Aunt Mimi brushed a hand across my cheek. "We might have been too late if you hadn't fi-nally used your gifts."

I hated to admit it, but I had forgotten I had a few tricks up my sleeve that could have helped me much earlier. Maybe that would come with time. "The next time I get into a sticky situation, I will follow Milo's advice and use my magic."

Gage had handed Meredith off to Peabody, who had shown up with another officer. Aunt Mimi, Nikki, and Nate took a step back and Milo squirmed out of my arms.

"Hey." I said and pulled my phone from my pocket. "I might have gotten her confession on audio."

He wrapped his arms around me and pulled me to his chest. "I was so scared she was going to hurt you."

I could feel his heart racing and I placed my hand on his chest, willing it to slow down. Much to my surprise, it began to return to a normal pace. Was that magic or just being close to me? Who knew, and I didn't care. All that mattered was Gage was safe.

"You know, the strangest thing happened in there." His deep voice was soothing to my jangled emotions.

"Oh?" Was he able to feel the spell?

"Yeah. Meredith was moving in my direction. The look in her eye told me she was going to stop at nothing to achieve her goal and that was going through me to get to you. Don't ask me how I knew, but I did. And then I got the strangest sensation and she veered off in the direction where I could see you."

"I was always her primary target, well, Flora was, and she mistook me for the former head librarian."

"No. She couldn't have seen you from where she was. But I saw you standing there with your eyes closed, talking to yourself. Why on earth would you have waited when you could have gotten out?"

Stepping away from the comfort of his arms, I looked up. "I would never have left you in harm's way. I was doing what I could to protect you."

"That's the nicest thing you've ever said. But closing your eyes wasn't the best way to help either of us."

One of these days I'd tell him the truth, that the whiteness that had enveloped him was the purist of love protecting him. But not tonight. For right now, I was going to linger a little longer in his arms.

The next night, Gage and I, along with Nikki and Steve, met at Aunt Mimi's house. Nate had promised to make lobster bisque and cheddar rolls for dinner. Of course, Nikki had whipped up a pie for the occasion, too. Me, I was all about grilling my aunt and her beau until they confessed their secret. I wasn't above using coercion to get what I wanted either.

We sat around the fire pit overlooking the ocean. The widow's walk was above us. Had it really only been two days since I learned the protection spell and cast it to save Gage? Aunt Mimi and Nikki had put a protection spell around me to save me from the fall and bashing from a metal bat. All in all, it was good to see magic was strong in our little town.

Gage touched my hand. "Can we talk about last night?"

I smiled. "I've been hoping you'd bring up the subject. Tell us what happened with Meredith."

"We have sent her to a psych hospital for an evaluation. It was obvious she had a break with reality. I would say from being bullied for so many years, it reached a breaking point. I heard from the doctor that she remembers what happened last night. More like it was a movie we all watched and not reality."

I nodded. My heart broke a little more for her. She'd had to endure so much with Flora, but now hopefully she'd get the help she desperately needed. "That's good news." I turned to my aunt and noticed she and Nate were holding hands. A sparkle of something caught my eye from her left hand. Was that a ring?

"Aunt Mimi, considering I almost died trying to protect you, I think the least you can do is tell me what your big secret is."

Nate gave her hand a squeeze. Of course I noticed, and he smiled at her with a nod. "I think you should tell them, mermaid. It's bound to come out sooner or later and you wanted us to control the news."

She sat up straight in the lawn chair. "I had wanted to do this during the celebration of the fall equinox, but since all of this has happened, Nate and I agree you should know. But I ask that you act surprised when I tell your parents."

I scooched forward in my chair, eager to hear what was going on. But after this buildup, my intuition was pinging. "Aunt Mimi, do I have a new uncle?"

Her mouth fell open, and she grinned while holding up their joined hands. "Meet your Uncle Nate."

"When?"

"Two months ago in Portland at city hall. We thought we'd just run off and make it legal and then tell the family and have a big party to celebrate in September. But Flora saw us coming down the stairs. Nate looked handsome in his blue suit, me in a cream-colored dress carrying a bouquet of the most beautiful roses in white, yellow, and red."

I breathed. "Just like the ones Flora had under her body."

Aunt Mimi's smile dimmed. "That night, she had a small bouquet of flowers on her desk and made sure I saw them. It was her way of adding more pressure to the situation between us. I wasn't budging, and she thought I'd cave. Obviously, she didn't know of our plans to tell everyone. But I would not let some nasty person get under my skin. So I turned the other cheek. But after she had left, I decided to give her a piece of my mind. I walked out of the library and the rest you know."

I sat back. Stunned. "She was a nervy woman." Everyone nodded in agreement. "I'm glad the case is solved and everyone is in the clear." I leaned back in my chair. "Do you think Marshall will get the courage to talk to Jill and tell her how he feels?"

Aunt Mimi gave her a reassuring smile. "Lily. Love always finds a way, even if it takes its own sweet time."

Gage tapped the arm of my chair. "Take a walk with me?"

I looked between Nikki and Aunt Mimi, who gave me a sly wink and a wide grin. I followed him down the rose-lined path to the rocky coastline. Was this it? Was Gage about to confess he had feelings for me?

We walked a short distance in companionable silence. He began, "I was terrified when this feeling came over me. You were in trouble. I got to the library as fast as I could, but things could have turned out very differently."

"We are both okay and that's all the matters."

Gage stopped walking and he looked me in the eye. "Promise me this was the last time you'll get involved in any kind of investigation and you'll leave it to the professionals."

"I had to help Mimi. There was no way I'd stand by, twiddling my thumbs, and let her get accused of a crime when she was innocent."

"I will always protect your family and you, but promise me, please?"

I started walking down the beach, picking up skimming stones and trying to skip them across the flat part of the waves. "How about we make a deal?"

He groaned. "I'm so not going to like this." But I could hear the laughter in his tone too.

"I promise that if I have the option to investigate a crime in Pembroke again, I will be much more careful."

He dropped his arm around my shoulders. "That's a relief since we live in a very safe town where the most exciting things that happen are jaywalkers and the occasional speeder."

I didn't have the heart to remind him of the obvious. We had just had a murder in our bucolic town and if my intuition was to be believed, which I've realized it should, something else was just around the corner.

If you loved Books & Bribes help other readers find this book: **Please leave a review now!**

Are you ready to read more about from the Lily and the gang in Pembroke?

Keep reading for a sneak peek at Catnip & Crimes, A Book Store Cozy Mystery Series
Order Now

Catnaps & Crimes

&

Crimes

A
BOOK STORE
COZY
MYSTERY

Book Two

LUCINDA RACE

Chapter 1 - Lily

I peeked out the front door of my bookshop, The Cozy Nook, right after I heard the nails on the chalkboard kind of grating but it was metal grinding on metal. A sound that jarred my last nerve. I had spent the last hour trying to perfect a levitation spell, to no avail.

"Milo," I called to my gray tabby cat. "Did you hear that?" If any customer had been in the shop, they'd assume I always talked to my cat like he understood, but in this case, he could. Milo was my familiar.

He slunk into the room. "What are you

yelling about? I was having a perfectly peaceful snooze in the sun."

No doubt on the kitchen counter again, but I didn't care. My space was his space. I had come to terms with the fact that we'd be together for life, even if he annoyed me at times. But that was bound to happen in the best of relationships. "There's been a car accident in the town square." I pulled open the door. "I'm going to make sure everyone is okay."

"Right. You want to investigate the scene of the accident."

I glared at him over my shoulder. "You say that like it's a bad thing."

"Lily, you're a witch, not a cop. Leave the mundane stuff to the police. Call your boyfriend, Gage."

I sighed the minute Milo mentioned Gage's name. "He's not my boyfriend. He's a friend who is a man." I slammed the door behind me and hurried over the brick sidewalk to where a late model sports car had veered into a metal flag pole at the edge of the town square. The driver couldn't have hit that dead center any better if there had been a bull's-eye on it.

A few shop owners and customers had come out of the different stores to see what had happened. From where I was standing, I could see inside the car. The driver was slumped against the steering wheel and on the cream-colored leather dashboard was a fast-growing pool of red. I looked over to Beatrice, who owned Bee Bee's Boutique and Tucker Ross from the hardware store. They were huddled together, pointing, talking, and watching. Jerilyn Busch was just going into the Sweet Spot, and Gretchen Wilson was frozen in place on the sidewalk. All around, locals were milling about, starting their day.

I shouted to anyone who would listen. "Call the police and tell them we need an ambulance. The driver looks to be hurt pretty bad." I refocused my attention on the car and driver. Smoke was drifting up from the engine compartment and I hoped that wasn't a sign a fire was brewing under the hood. I could light a candle but didn't have any idea how to put a fire out. New witch here. I tried the door handle, but the door was locked or jammed. Then I tapped on the glass. Again, the driver didn't move and I couldn't tell if he was awake. His dark-brown fedora was pulled low, obscuring his face. I ran around the back of the car and attempted to open the passenger door, but I noticed the front fender was jammed back against the door. There was no way I was going to open it.

The wail of sirens was growing closer, and I hoped Gage was coming too. Even though he was a detective and not just a cop, he had a calming influence on everyone, including me. I beat on the driver's window again. "Hey, you need to get out of the car." The wisps of smoke were getting bigger. What if the car burst into flames? The shops nearby could be in danger. I closed my eyes. Did any of the spells I had learned work in this situation? Would the protection spell be effective? So far I had only tried it on my Aunt Mimi when she was the prime suspect in a murder investigation of the former head librarian, and then Gage when the assistant librarian was zeroing in on him after she had a break with reality. She was out to harm Gage and of course me too.

In the brief moments I was alone, I tried to decide how best to throw up a protection spell for the buildings and people. Finally, the fire truck, two police cars, an ambulance, and a dark-colored sedan rolled up, all parking at odd angles as if surrounding the scene from prying eyes.

"Gage!" I yelled. "It's smoking." I pointed to the hood of the car.

"Lily, are you okay?"

I was relieved to see his tall, well-built frame headed in my direction. It was sweet. His first concern was for me and not the accident victim, but after what we had been through a few weeks ago with the murder investigation, I surmised it was to be expected. "I'm fine, but the driver is another story." I jabbed a finger in that direction. "I've knocked on the glass, tried to open the doors, but no luck. There's so much blood."

He called to the firefighters and waved his

hands in the smoke's direction. "We need the jaws of life and be prepared for an engine fire."

Emergency personnel sprang into action. I moved to the sidewalk, away from the controlled chaos. The whine of machinery pried open the driver's door, and fire suppressant blanketed the engine compartment. I watched as Officers Peabody and Sullivan questioned the group of onlookers, trying to determine if anyone had actually seen the accident happen. I noticed Ross Frederick coming down the street, and when he saw the car, he froze and hurried in the opposite direction.

Gage had stepped to one side and was on his cell phone. His light-brown hair dipped over his eyes. The worried expression on his face conveyed the seriousness. Several tense minutes later, the door was yanked from the car.

Two EMTs rushed forward. The first leaned in. I could see her mouth moving, but I was too far away to hear what she was saying. She eased the person back against the seat, then pressed her fingers to his neck and pulled out a stethoscope and placed the round disc against his chest. She leaned in closer and then withdrew. "Detective Erikson?"

Gage held up his finger, showing he'd be another minute. He said a few more words and then put his phone into his jacket pocket. This was the first time I noticed I was chilled to the bone. I rubbed my hands over my arms, all the while keeping an eye on Gage and the person who had checked over the driver. Dang it, I wished I had super hearing or better, a spell that would help me hear conversations at a distance. I'd have to consult my book, *Practical Beginnings*, to see if such a thing existed.

The expression on Gage's face didn't change, but in his hazel eyes, I saw the truth. I could tell the news was grim. He nodded twice. In addition, based on the fact that no one else was taking care of the man, it had been a tragic turn of events and the car crash took a person's life.

Peabody crossed the grass to where I was waiting. Her dark hair was pulled back in a low bun at the base of her police hat. Her uniform was pressed and her shoes were freshly shined. "Lily. I hear you were first at the scene. Will you tell me what you saw?"

"How are you, Sharon?" She had only been on the force a short while and as far as I knew, no one called her by her given name except me. She seemed to prefer Peabody.

"I'm fine. Now can you tell me what you saw?" Her words came out clipped, and she held her small notepad out, pen poised, ready to capture my every word.

My eyes stayed on the car, or what was left of it. "I heard the sound of metal on metal. The crash. I ran out and went to the driver's door, tapped on the glass, and asked if he was okay. When he didn't answer and I couldn't get the door open, I tried the other side. Same result. At that point, I heard the sirens, and you all arrived."

"Did you see any other cars, like someone who might have been involved in the crash?"

I shook my head and wrapped my stiff arms around my body. I started to shiver. "No. When

I came out, there wasn't even anyone on the sidewalk. It was just the car."

She nodded, jotted something down, and closed her pad. "If you think of anything else, you'll call the police station?"

Peabody posed it as a question, since I had a tiny bit of a reputation for investigating things I shouldn't. It wasn't really my fault. I loved puzzles and had a burning desire to find the answers. "Of course I will."

She quirked a brow as if challenging the validity of that statement, but didn't respond before walking away. The low heels of her dark boots didn't make a sound on the brick sidewalk, and she had her hand on the butt of her firearm, as if keeping it secured.

Gage walked over to me. "How are you doing?"

His tall, muscular frame towered over me, but his height made me feel safe. I shrugged. "Okay." A shiver raced down my spine, as much from the cold as something else. But I couldn't put my finger on what. Possibly my intuition, but why would that be poking at me? This was an unfortunate accident.

Gage slipped his jacket off and wrapped it around my shoulders. "That should help."

I noticed the license plate on the car. Maine. But no one I knew locally drove a fancy sports car. It was impractical with the amount of snow we received each winter. But they could store it and have something else to drive. "Any idea who the driver is?"

"Detective Erikson. A moment, please?" Mac Sullivan, the other police officer, called to him and gestured for Gage to come back to the car.

"Why don't you get back inside and I'll come over to the shop before I take off?"

I went to hand him the jacket, and he said, "Keep it. I'll get it later."

He was a sweet man and that familiar pang of wishing for something, namely Gage in my life, lingered in my heart. "I'll put on some tea."

He touched my arm and my heart skipped before he jogged to where Mac and Peabody were waiting for him. My gaze went back to the car, where the poor driver was still belted into the seat. The smoke had evaporated, and I figured a wrecker would be called to remove the car. That poor man. I didn't look back as I crossed the street to my shop.

I placed a hand on the doorknob and was about to turn it when I saw Dax Peters striding down the sidewalk. His tall, thin frame had grown downright skinny over the last few weeks. We had met him for the first time when he came into my shop, declaring that Aunt Mimi was innocent of killing Flora Gray. Of course, he was right, but what was he doing here and why now?

I stepped inside the shop and watched from the window. He made a beeline for Gage, Peabody, and Mac. An animated conversation ensued, and Dax strode to the car. He walked around the outside and leaned into the now doorless driver's side. He looked at the driver but didn't move the hat back from his face. Then he seemed to take a long look around the interior before straightening up.

I kept a sharp eye on him. What did he see? Dax looked at my shop. His eyes seemed to bore into mine and I got the distinct impression he had just told me to keep my nose out of his investigation. A prickling sensation spread down my arms. Investigation?

I knew from watching Netflix crime shows that car accidents didn't warrant a fancy law enforcement person to look into things. It was the local police department that handled those mundane details. The only time they brought in the heavy hitters was when something hinky had been going on.

Gage walked to Dax, and they both looked toward my shop. Gage shook his head, and I hoped he was defending me from this interloper. All I knew about Dax was he showed up in Pembroke, said he had friends in town, and he'd be here for a little longer. But it had been almost a month and in my book that was not a short time. Especially since it wasn't tourist season any longer. But there must be something about this accident that wasn't normal. I had to know what it could be.

Milo jumped up on the windowsill next to me. "What did you find out? Someone driving too fast and crashed into the pole?" He began to lick his paw, completely unconcerned for the happenings outside the shop. "Those fancy cars fold like sardine cans." He looked up at me. "You know I've been such a good help mastering a few spells. How about I get a can of sardines as a treat?"

I couldn't help but snort. "It's been three weeks and I still haven't mastered the levitation spell, so no sardines for you until I do."

He growled like a lion, which I still found unnerving that he could do that. "Maybe my witch needs to spend more time practicing and less time drooling over Detective Cutie over there." He hopped down and trotted off in the direction of the back room.

I didn't have the chance to protest that I didn't drool over Gage and Milo should really stop calling him Detective Cutie. Where had that even come from? Certainly nothing I had said.

A movement caught my eye. Jill Dilly was running across the town square, her arms waving in the air as she called to Gage. He met her halfway between the car accident and my shop. And she stopped. I could see her chest was heaving as if she had run quite a distance.

I cracked open the shop door and turned my head with my ear directed toward them. With any luck, I could hear part of the conversation, if not all.

"Detective, who was driving that car?" She leaned around him, straining to catch a glimpse of the wreck.

"Jill. We haven't made a positive ID yet and until we do, we're not releasing any information. We have to contact the family first."

"It's Teddy Roberts, isn't it?"

My mouth fell open, and I snapped it shut before I could burst out a comment that no one needed to hear.

"Jill. When I can tell you something, I promise to call you. For now, please go home."

He gently turned Jill back in the direction she came from. Seeming to vacillate between doing what he said and her wanting to know, he pointed to where her car must be. "I promise I'll be in touch."

Her shoulders sagged and with a catch in her voice, she said, "I know that's Teddy's car."

Gage looked at me. I didn't care that he caught me listening. He turned to come into the shop and I opened the door wide. When he came inside, and I took his jacket off and handed it to him.

"Before you ask, I'm going to tell you." He gave me a sharp look. "But this doesn't give you carte blanche to investigate."

I slowly nodded. "It was Teddy in the car?"

"It was."

"Poor guy, to die in a stupid car accident."

Gage's face was grim. "Teddy Roberts was dead before he hit the pole. He had been shot."

A Free Story for You

Have you enjoyed Books & Bribes? Not ready to stop reading yet? If you sign up for my newsletter at www.lucindarace.com/newsletter you will received Blends, the love story of Sam and Sherry, right away as my thank-you gift for choosing to get my newsletter.

Can two hearts blend together for a life long love..

His mother's final illness waylaid Sam Price's college dreams, but he's content working in his

323

family's vineyard in a small town in upstate New York. When he finds a woman with a flat tire on a vineyard road, he's stunned to discover it's the girl he'd had a crush on in high school. He'd never been confident enough to ask her out back then. He'd been a farm kid. Her daddy was the bank president. Way out of his league.

Sherry Jones is tired of her parents' ambitious plans for her life. She'll finish her college accounting degree like they want, but how can she tell them about her real love: working with growing things? Then a flat tire and a neglected garden offer her an unexpected opportunity, with the added bonus of a tall, gorgeous guy with eyes that set her senses tingling.

What does a guy with dirt under his nails and calluses on his hands have to offer a woman like Sherry? It will take courage for her to defy her parents and claim her own dreams. Sam and Sherry's lives took different paths, but a winding vineyard road has brought them back together.

Are they willing to take a chance to create the perfect blend for a lifelong love?

Blends is only available by signing up for my newsletter – sign up for it here at <u>www.lucin</u> <u>darace.com/newsletter</u>

Love to read?

Cozy Mystery Books
A Bookstore Cozy Mystery Series
Books & Bribes

It was an ordinary day until the book of Practical Magic conked Lily on the head causing her to see stars. And then she discovered her cat, Milo, could talk.

Catnip & Crimes May 2023
The fun continues as Lily practices her magic and needs to investigate another murder.

Love to read?

Tea & Trouble August 2023
A fall festival and reading tea leave and just enough to propel Lily into a new murder investigation.

Scares & Dares October 2023

Cowboys of River Junction

Stars Over Montana
The cowboy broke her heart but he never stopped loving her. Now she's back ready to run her grandfather's ranch...

Hiding in Montana

Orchard Brides Series
Apple Blossoms in Montana
Twenty years later Renee and Hank are back where they fell in love but reality is like a spring frost and is a long-distance relationship their only option for their second chance?

Love to read?

The Sandy Bay Series
<u>Sundaes on Sunday</u>
A widowed school teacher and the airline pilot whose little girl is determined to bring her daddy and the lady from the ice cream shop together for a second chance at love.

Last Man Standing/Always a Bridesmaid
<u>Barrett</u>
Has the last man standing finally met his match?

<u>Marie</u> *May 2023*
Career focused city girl discovers small town charm can lead to love.

The Crescent Lake Winery Series
<u>Breathe</u>
Her dream come true may be the end of his...
Crush
The first time they met was fleeting, the second time restarted her heart.
<u>Blush</u>

Love to read?

He's always loved her but he left and now he's back...the question, does she still love him?

<u>Vintage</u>

He's an unexpected distraction, she gets his engine running...

<u>Bouquet</u>

Sweet second chances for a widow and the handsome billionaire...

Holiday Romance
<u>The Sugar Plum Inn</u>

The chef and the restaurant critic are about to come face to face.

Last Chance Beach
<u>Shamrocks are a Girl's Best Friend</u>

Will a bit of Irish luck and a matchmaking uncle give Kelly and Tric a chance to find love?

A Dickens Holiday Romance
<u>Holiday Heart Wishes</u>

Heartfelt wishes and holiday kisses...

<u>Holly Berries and Hockey Pucks</u>

Love to read?

Hockey, holidays, and a slap shot to the heart.

Christmas in July
She's the hometown girl with the hometown advantage. Right?

A Secret Santa Christmas
Christmas just isn't Holly's thing, but will a family secret help her find the true meaning of Christmas?

It's Just Coffee Series 2020
The Matchmaker and The Marine
She vowed never to love again. His career in the Marines crushed his ability to love. Can undeniable chemistry and a leap of faith overcome their past?

The MacLellan Sisters Trilogy
Old and New
An enchanted heirloom wedding dress and a letter change three sisters lives forever as they fulfill their grandmothers last request try on the

dress.

<u>Borrowed</u>

He's just a borrowed boyfriend. He might also be her true love.

<u>Blue</u>

Will an enchanted wedding dress work its magic one more time?

The Loudon Series

<u>Between Here and Heaven</u>

Ten years of heaven on earth dissolved in an instant for Cari McKenna when her husband Ben died.

<u>Lost and Found</u>

Love never ends... A widow who talks to her late husband and her handsome single neighbor who has secretly loved her for years.

<u>The Journey Home</u>

Where do you go to heal your heart? You make the journey home...

<u>The Last First Kiss</u>

When life handed Kate lemons, she baked.

<u>Ready to Soar</u>

Love to read?

Kate will fight for love, won't she?
<u>Love in the Looking Glass</u>
*Will Ellie's first love be her last or will she
become a ghost like her father?*
<u>Magic in the Rain</u>
*Dani's plan of hiding in plain sight may not have
been the best idea.*

Social Media

Follow Me on Social Media

Like my Facebook page
Join Lucinda's Heart Racer's Reader Group on
Facebook
Twitter @lucindarace
Instagram @lucindraceauthor
BookBub
Goodreads
Pinterest

About the Author

Award-winning and best-selling author Lucinda Race is a lifelong fan of reading. As a young girl, she spent hours reading novels and getting lost in the fun and hope they represent. While her friends dreamed of becoming doctors and engineers, her dreams were to become a writer—a novelist.

As life twisted and turned, she found herself writing nonfiction but longed to turn to her true passion. After developing the storyline for A McKenna Family Romance, it was time to start living her dream. Her fingers practically fly over computer keys as she weaves stories of mystery and romance.

Lucinda lives with her two little dogs, a miniature long hair dachshund and a shih tzu mix rescue, in the rolling hills of western Massachusetts. When she's not at her day job, she's immersed in her fictional worlds. And if she's not writing romance or cozy mystery novels, she's reading everything she can get her hands on.

Printed in the USA
CPSIA information can be obtained
at www.ICGtesting.com
LVHW010748241123
764806LV00047B/1299

9 781954 520561